3 Tony® Award N...
3 Outer Critics Circle...
9 Drama Desk N...

MADE IN AMERICA

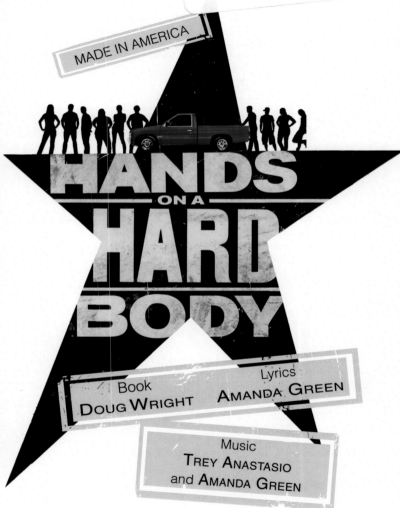

HANDS ON A HARD BODY

Book
DOUG WRIGHT

Lyrics
AMANDA GREEN

Music
TREY ANASTASIO
and AMANDA GREEN

SAMUEL FRENCH

Samuel French, Inc.   Samuel French Ltd.
45 West 25th Street   52 Fitzroy Street
New York, NY 10010   London W1T 5JR England

www.SamuelFrench.com   www.SamuelFrench-London.co.uk

FOR PRODUCTION INQUIRIES
Info@SamuelFrench.com
1-866-598-8449

RENTAL MATERIALS

An orchestration consisting of **Piano/Conductor/Keyboard 1**, **Keyboard 2/Organ**, **Guitar/Mandolin**, **Guitar 2**, **Bass**, **Drums**, **Violin**, and **Cello** will be loaned two months prior to the production ONLY on the receipt of the Licensing Fee quoted for all performances, the rental fee and a refundable deposit.

Samphony™ Rehearsal and Performance Accompaniment Tracks are available to licensees upon request. Additional rental fees will apply.

Please contact Samuel French for perusal of the music materials as well as a performance license application.

IMPORTANT BILLING AND CREDIT REQUIREMENTS

All producers of *HANDS ON A HARDBODY must* give credit to the Author(s) of the Play(s) in all programs distributed in connection with performances of the Play(s), and in all instances in which the title of the Play(s) appears for the purposes of advertising, publicizing or otherwise exploiting the Play(s) and/or a production. The name of the Author(s) *must* appear on a separate line on which no other name appears, immediately following the title and *must* appear in size of type not less than fifty percent of the size of the title type.

Additional billing and credit requirements, specific to licensed productions, can be found in the Samuel French licensing agreement.

PLAYWRIGHT'S NOTE

Americans thrive on competition; it's innate in our character. Every summer in Spivey's Corner, North Carolina, they hold the National Hollerin' Contest. On Independence Day, Coney Island plays host to Nathan's Famous hot dog eating challenge. Lawn Mower Racing is an established sport in the South, and the annual Redneck Games in Georgia feature hubcap hurling, toilet seat tosses, and mud-pit belly flopping.

In the mid-1990s, documentarian S.R. Bindler captured the Hands on a Hardbody competition in Longview, Texas. In it, contestants placed their hands on a new Nissan "Hardbody" pick-up truck; the entrant who could stand the longest without removing his or her hand from the vehicle won it. The contest garnered international exposure and launched a host of similar promotions across the country. Filmmaker Bindler's achievement lies in his ability to push past the kitschy, absurd premise of the event and hit on deeper truths about the duality of the American Dream. On one hand, anyone with skill and perseverance can triumph, but beneath that bright promise lies a darker one: Darwin's cruel truth about the survival of the fittest.

Amanda Green, Trey Anastasio and I felt the film was ripe for theatrical adaptation. We believe it's more relevant today than it was upon its release; our recent economic tumult has brought age-old fissures of race, class and income inequality to the fore. The truck brings disparate individuals together, who would otherwise never meet, to confront these issues with a startling directness. Implicit in the contest is the American myth of mobility, embodied by an automobile. The truck offers plenty of metaphors; for one contestant, it's a new lease on life; for another, it's his manhood; for a third, it's her religious faith.

For me, the show is a chance to explore my roots in a state that's simultaneously maddening and exhilarating, punch-drunk on its own rich mythology, tongue-in-cheek braggadocio, abundant good humor and boundless sky. For Amanda and Trey, it's an opportunity to forge a score inspired by doggedly individualistic, real-life people and musical idioms from country ballads to southern rock, Americana, swampy funk, gospel and delta blues. We wrote the play in venues across the nation: a writer's retreat in Wyoming, a barn in Vermont and Interstate 20 between Dallas and Shreveport. It all culminated in a premiere run at San Diego's La Jolla Playhouse in the summer of 2012. It's been a joyous enterprise, and now we're on Broadway. It's our portrait of America; we hope it strikes a chord.

–Doug Wright

HANDS ON A HARDBODY had its Broadway premiere at the Brooks Atkinson Theatre in New York City on March 21, 2013. The performance was directed by Neil Pepe and choreographed by Sergio Trujillo, with sets by Christine Jones, costumes by Susan Hilferty, lighting by Kevin Adams, sound design by Steve Canyon Kennedy, and orchestrations by Trey Anastasio and Don Hart. The Production Stage Manager was Linda Marvel.

The Broadway premiere was originally produced by Broadway Across America: Beth Williams, Barbara Whitman, Latitude Link, Dede Harris, Sharon Karmazin, and Howard & Janet Kagan. Additional producers include John & Claire Caudwell, Rough Edged Souls, Joyce Primm Schweickert, Paula Black, Bruce Long, Off the Aisle Productions, and Freitag-Mishkin.

The cast for the Brodway production was as follows (alphabetical order):

CAST

J.D.	Keith Carradine
KELLI	Allison Case
BENNY	Hunter Foster
GREG	Jay Armstrong Johnson
CHRIS	David Larsen
RONALD	Jacob Ming-Trent
HEATHER	Kathleen Elizabeth Monteleone
VIRGINIA	Mary Gordon Murray
MIKE	Jim Newman
CINDY	Connie Ray
JESUS	Jon Rua
NORMA	Keala Settle
JANIS	Dale Soules
FRANK	Scott Wakefield
DON/DR. STOKES	William Youmans

HANDS ON A HARDBODY had its world premiere at La Jolla Playhouse in La Jolla, California on May 12, 2012. The Artistic Director was Christopher Ashley. The Managing Director was Michael S. Rosenberg.

HANDS ON A HARDBODY is based on the Documentary Film by S. R. Bindler and Kevin Morris, HOHB Production, LLC.

BROADWAY CAST

KEITH CARRADINE *(JD Drew).* Broadway: *Hair, Foxfire* (OCC Award), *The Will Rogers Follies* (Tony nomination), *Dirty Rotten Scoundrels.* Off-Broadway: *Wake Up, It's Time to Go to Bed; Mindgame; A Lie of the Mind.* Regional: *Another Part of the Forest, Detective Story, Stuff Happens, New Year's Eve.* Films include *McCabe and Mrs. Miller, Emperor of the North, Thieves Like Us, Nashville* (Academy Award, Composer, Best Song, "I'm Easy"), *The Duellists, Pretty Baby, Choose Me, The Long Riders, Southern Comfort, The Moderns, Cowboys and Aliens, Ain't Them Bodies Saints.* TV includes "Deadwood," "Dexter," "Crash," "Damages," "Missing."

ALLISON CASE *(Kelli Mangrum)* is so grateful to be here after playing Kelli in the La Jolla Playhouse production! Broadway: *Mamma Mia!* (Sophie); originated the role of Crissy in the Tony Award-winning revival of *Hair* (Off-Broadway, Broadway, West End). Also Nemo in *Finding Nemo: The Musical* (Disney); *Por Quinly and The Only Child* (South Coast Repertory). Workshops: *The Book of Mormon, Hands on a Hardbody, Hadestown, Dogfight.* TV: "Nurse Jackie," "NYC 22." Film: *The Blue Eyes, Patient 001.* UC Irvine graduate. Couldn't be here without Mom, Dad, Parker, Ashley, family, friends. LOVE!

HUNTER FOSTER *(Benny Perkins).* Broadway: *Million Dollar Quartet, The Producers, Little Shop of Horrors* (Tony, Drama Desk, Outer Critics noms.), *Urinetown* (Outer Critics nom.), *Les Misérables, Grease, Footloose, King David.* Off-Broadway: *Borrowed Dust, Burning, Ordinary Days, Happiness* (Drama Desk nom.), *Frankenstein, Dust, Modern Orthodox, Urinetown* (Lortel nom.). Regional: *Hands on a Hardbody* (La Jolla), *Little Miss Sunshine* (La Jolla), *Kiss of the Spider Woman* (Signature Theatre, Helen Hayes nom.), *The Government Inspector* (Guthrie), *Mister Roberts* (Kennedy Center). He is currently appearing as Scotty Simms on the ABC Family show "Bunheads."

JAY ARMSTRONG JOHNSON *(Greg Wilhote)*. Broadway: *Catch Me If You Can (Frank Jr. Standby)*, *Hair* (original revival cast, Claude u/s). Off-B'way: *Wild Animals You Should Know* (MCC), *Working* (Prospect). First national tour: *A Chorus Line* (Mark). Regional: *Pirates!* (Frederick), MUNY; *Hands on a Hardbody* (Greg), La Jolla; *Pool Boy* (Nick), Barrington; *Hairspray* (Link), Weston; *West Side Story* (Baby John), Casa Mañana. Also *35mm: A Musical Exhibition* (on iTunes). TV/film: *Sex and the City 2*, "Law & Order: SVU," "The Apprentice." Texas forever! @Jay_A_Johnson

DAVID LARSEN *(Chris Alvaro)*. Broadway: *American Idiot* (Tunny); *Billy Elliot* (Tony u/s), original cast; *Good Vibrations* (Bobby), original cast. TV: "Boston Public." Regional: Principals at Hollywood Bowl, Glimmerglass Opera, Bay Street, Goodspeed, Marriott Lincolnshire, Pittsburgh CLO, KC Starlight. BFA, Carnegie Mellon. Love to Amanda and family. @dlarsen22

JACOB MING-TRENT *(Ronald McCowan)*. Broadway: *Shrek the Musical* (original cast). Off-Broadway: *The Merchant of Venice* (TFANA), *On the Levee* (Lincoln Center), *Widowers' Houses* (Epic Theatre Ensemble), *Dispatches* (E.T.E.). Tours: *Putnam County Spelling Bee*, *Two Gentlemen of Verona*. NY, London, regional: Playwrights Horizons, the Public Theater, Barbican Theatre, Yale Rep, New Georges, McCarter Theatre, Dallas Theater Center, A.C.T., Berkeley Rep, Long Wharf, La Jolla Playhouse, etc. TV: "L&O," "Bored to Death," "Unforgettable," "30 Rock." Films: *Forbidden Love, Fort Greene*.

KATHLEEN ELIZABETH MONTELEONE *(Heather Stovall)* most recently played Heather Stovall in *Hands on a Hardbody* at La Jolla Playhouse. Other credits include Dede Halcyon-Day in *Tales of the City* (American Conservatory Theater), the national tour of *Legally Blonde the Musical* (Elle Woods/Ensemble), Sophie in *Departure Lounge* (SPF)

and Amber in *Hairspray* (Paper Mill Playhouse). Screen credits include NBC's "Grease: You're the One That I Want" (Spiritual Sandy) and the film *27 Dresses*. A graduate of Marymount Manhattan College. Love to my family and Frank. Kathleenmonteleone.com

 **MARY GORDON MURRAY** (*Virginia Drew*). Credits include Virginia, *Hands on a Hardbody*, La Jolla Playhouse. Broadway: the Baker's Wife in *Into the Woods*, Belle in *Little Me* (Tony nomination, Best Actress), *Footloose*, *Coastal Disturbances*, *Grease*, *Play Me a Country Song*, *I Love My Wife*, *The Robber Bridegroom*. Off-Broadway: *The Spitfire Grill*, *A...My Name Is Alice*, *The Knife*. Television: Laura Bush in "DC 9/11," Becky on "One Life to Live." Guest starring/recurring: "L.A. Law" to "The Ghost Whisperer." Feature films: *Poison Ivy, Born Yesterday*, and *Junior*.

 **JIM NEWMAN** (*Mike Ferris*). Broadway: *Curtains* (Parson Tuck), *Minnelli on Minnelli*, *Steel Pier* (Happy), *Sunset Boulevard* and The Who's *Tommy*. Encores!: *On a Clear Day You Can See Forever* (Millard). 1st national tours: *Kiss Me, Kate* (Bill Calhoun); *Big* (Josh Baskin); and *Joseph...Dreamcoat* (Levi). Off-Broadway: *Lucky Guy, Almost Heaven, Newsical!, A Good Swift Kick*, and *Up Against It*. Television: "Hope and Faith," "All My Children," "One Life to Live," "The Rosie O'Donnell Show," and "The Magic of Music." Film: *The Big Gay Musical, Out of Sync*.

 **CONNIE RAY** (*Cindy Barnes*). Broadway: *Next Fall, The Heidi Chronicles*. Off-Broadway: *Next Fall, Smoke on the Mountain* (which she also wrote), among others. OOB: *Fast Eddie, Forgetting Frankie, Catfish Loves Anna*. Film: *Flags of Our Fathers, Thank You for Smoking, About Schmidt, Ice Princess, Hope Floats, Stuart Little, The Time Machine, Idle Hands, My Fellow Americans*. TV: "The Torkelsons," "The Big C," "Law & Order: SVU," "Hart of Dixie," "Justified," "Entourage," "Worst Week," "George Lopez," and "My Name Is Earl."

JON RUA (*Jesus Peña*). Broadway: Sonny in *In the Heights*. Off-Broadway: *The Elaborate Entrance of Chad Deity* (Second Stage), *Damn Yankees* (City Center Encores!). Regional: Alejandro in *Somewhere* (Old Globe, Craig Noel nom.), Twig in *Bring It On* (Alliance), *Pirates!* (MUNY). Workshops: *Hands on a Hardbody* (La Jolla), Sundance Theatre Lab, Stardust Ballroom, Kingdom (Public Theater), Lincoln Center's American Songbook. TV: "Law & Order". Choreography: Broadway Bares, NBA, Union Square. Assistant: *Hardbody, Flashdance, In the Heights, Bring It On,* NYCC's *The Wiz, Insanity.* For Mom and Dad. www.JonRua.net

KEALA SETTLE (*Norma Valverde*). Nau Mai Haere Mai! Thank you for supporting live theatre by being here tonight! Much mahalo to the creative team, Bernie and Craig, Rachel Hoffman, DGRW and this entire company for their patience and love and for humbling me everyday. This one's for my whanau and the Block. Any other questions can be directed google.com. It will set you free! Enjoy!

DALE SOULES (*Janis Curtis*), aka Dances With Trucks. Broadway: *Hair* (debut), *Dude, The Magic Show* (introducing Stephen Schwartz's songs "Lion Tamer" and "West End Avenue"), *Whose Life Is It Anyway?, The Crucible* (Richard Eyre, director), *Grey Gardens* (Michael Greif, director). Off-Broadway, regional and international credits are extensive, from Marsha Norman's *Getting Out* (NY) to Candide (Guthrie) to the Builders Association's *Jet Lag* (Barbican). TV and film includes Maurice Sendack's "Really Rosie," "Law & Order," and *The Messenger.* Thanks Doug Wright and NYTW. www.dalesoules.com

SCOTT WAKEFIELD (*Frank Nugent*). Broadway: *It Ain't Nothin' But the Blues, Ring of Fire.* Off-Broadway: *The Joy Luck Club, The American Clock, Golden Boy of the Blue Ridge.* Regional: Milwaukee Repertory, Seattle Repertory, Cincinnati Playhouse, Alliance Theatre, Missouri Repertory, La Jolla Playhouse, Delaware Theatre Company, O'Neill Center,

Williamstown Festival, Asolo Theatre Company, Spoleto Festival, among others. Best Actor awards: *The Will Rogers Follies*, *Woody Guthrie's American Song, Best Little Whorehouse....* Two original CDs: Vegetarian Nightmare and Older Than Dirt are available at ScottWakefield.com.

WILLIAM YOUMANS (*Don Curtis/Dr. Stokes*). Broadway original casts: *Wicked, The Little Foxes* (Elizabeth Taylor), *Big River, The Farnsworth Invention, Titanic, Finian's Rainbow,* Baz Luhrmann's *La Bohème, The Pirate Queen, Billy Elliot.* Off-Broadway: *Giant* (Public), *Road Show* (Public, Sondheim), *Brundibar* (Kushner), *Coraline* (MCC), *The Widow Claire* (Horton Foote). Film/TV: *Extremely Loud & Incredibly Close, Mrs. Soffel, Compromising Positions, Nadine, A League of Their Own,* "666 Park Avenue" (recurring), "The Little Match Girl," "Separate But Equal," "Private History" (Peabody Award).

CREATIVE TEAM

DOUG WRIGHT (*Book*) was born in Dallas, 120 miles from Longview, Texas. Broadway: *I Am My Own Wife* (Pulitzer Prize, Tony Award), *Grey Gardens* (Tony nomination), *The Little Mermaid.* Film: *Quills,* based on his Obie-winning play, nominated for three Academy Awards. Television: "Tony Bennett: An American Classic", directed by Rob Marshall. Honors: Benjamin Dank Prize, the American Academy of Arts and Letters; Tolerance Prize, Kulturforum Europa; Paul Selvin Award, Writers Guild of America. Professional affiliations: Dramatists Guild, Society of Stage Directors and Choreographers, board of the New York Theatre Workshop. Doug is married to singer/songwriter David Clement.

AMANDA GREEN (*Lyrics and Music*) is thrilled to see *Hands on a Hardbody* come to Broadway. She had the good fortune to have a second musical, *Bring It On,* premiere on Broadway this season after its successful national tour (LADCC nomination, Best Score; GLAAD nomination). Also on Broadway: *High Fidelity* (lyrics). Regional: *Hallelujah*

Baby! (additional lyrics; Arena Stage, dir. Arthur Laurents); *For the Love of Tiffany* (lyrics, co-star; NY Fringe Festival). Awards: Jonathan Larson Award, Songwriters Hall of Fame Scholarship. Amanda performs her songs everywhere from Birdland to the Bluebird Café in Nashville, and has won two MAC Awards. Trey Anastasio performs their songs with his bands Phish and TAB. She is married to Dr. Jeffrey Kaplan.

TREY ANASTASIO (*Music and Orchestrations*) was born in Fort Worth, Texas. He is a founding member of Phish. Trey has received Grammy nominations for his work with Phish, as well as his solo albums and his 2005 collaboration with Herbie Hancock. Named by *Rolling Stone* as one of the 100 Greatest Guitarists of All Time, Trey has also performed original compositions with numerous symphonies, including the New York Philharmonic. He has long aspired to work in musical theatre, and *Hands on a Hardbody* marks his first Broadway musical. His latest solo album, "Traveler", was released in 2012. Trey lives in Manhattan with his wife Sue and his two daughters, Eliza and Bella.

NEIL PEPE (*Director*). Broadway credits include the acclaimed revival of *Speed-the-Plow* and David Mamet's *A Life in the Theatre.* Off-Broadway: Jez Butterworth's *Parlour Song, Mojo* and *The Night Heron*; Ethan Coen's *Happy Hour, Offices* and *Almost an Evening*; Harold Pinter's *Celebration* and *The Room*; Adam Rapp's *Dreams of Flying, Dreams of Falling*; David Pittu's *What's That Smell?*; Howard Korder's *Sea of Tranquility* (all at Atlantic); David Mamet's *American Buffalo* (Donmar Warehouse, Atlantic); *Romance, Keep Your Pantheon/School* (Center Theatre Group, Atlantic); Jessica Goldberg's *Refuge* (Playwrights Horizons); Tom Donaghy's *The Beginning of August* (South Coast Repertory, Atlantic). Also, Frank Gilroy's *The Subject Was Roses* with Martin Sheen (CTG). Since 1992, Neil has been the artistic director of the award-winning Off-Broadway company, Atlantic Theater Company.

SERJIO TRUJILLO (*Choreographer*). Tony Award Best Musical, *Memphis* (OCC Award, Astaire, Drama Desk Award noms.); Tony/Olivier Award Best Musical, *Jersey Boys* (Drama Desk, Dora, OCC Award nominations, Green Room Award); *Leap of Faith* (Drama Desk, Astaire nominations); *The Addams*

Family; *Next To Normal* (Lucille Lortel Award nomination); *All Shook Up*; *Guys and Dolls* (Astair Award nomination). Director/ Choreographer: *Flashdance*. Off-Broadway: *Saved*; *The Capeman*, *Romeo and Juliet* (Public); *A Tree Grows in Brooklyn*, *Kismet* (Encores!); *Salome* (NYC Opera). Also *White Noise* (Director/Choreographer); *The Wiz*, *Zhivago* (La Jolla); *Mambo Kings*; *The Marriage of Figaro* (LA Opera); *Chita and All That Jazz*. Ovation Award for Empire: A New American Musical, four Dora Award nominations.

S.R. BINDLER (*Creator/Producer of Original Documentary*). S.R. Bindler's *Hands on a Hardbody* continues to be a cult hit a decade after its initial release. It won AFI's Best Documentary Award, numerous film-festival and critic's honors and was a smash hit to sold-out audiences coast-to-coast. His national commercial work has won ADDY and Andy awards and has honored by the AICP.

KEVIN MORRIS (*Producer of Original Documentary*). Founder of Entertainment law firm Morris Yorn. In addition to *Hands on a Hardbody*, he has produced a number of independent films and is currently producing and co-writing the screenplay for *Dictablanda*. His business writing has appeared in the *Wall Street Journal* and *LA Times*. He is also a co-producer of *The Book of Mormon*.

CARMEL DEAN (*Musical Director and Vocal Arranger*). Broadway: *American Idiot* (Musical Director), *The 25th Annual Putnam County Spelling Bee* (Vocal Arranger/Associate Conductor). Off-Broadway: *Everyday Rapture* and *Elegies: A Song Cycle*. Regional and international: *Tales of the City* (ACT), *Chicago* (Hong Kong) and the 2000 Sydney Olympics Opening/Closing Ceremonies. Other: "The 52nd Annual Grammy Awards" (with Green Day). Fulbright Scholar and graduate of NYU's Musical Theatre Writing Program. Made in Australia! Original songs at www.carmeldean.com.

CHRISTINE JONES (*Scenic Design*). Broadway: *American Idiot* (Tony Award), *Everyday Rapture*, *Spring Awakening* (Tony nomination), all directed by Michael Mayer; *The Green Bird*, with director Julie Taymor (Drama Desk nomination). Off-Broadway includes *Coraline* (Lucille Lortel); *The Book of Longing*, music by Phillip Glass, based on the poems of Leonard Cohen (Lincoln Center Festival). She recently designed *Rigoletto* for the Metropolitan Opera. She is the artistic director of Theatre for One, and is an adjunct faculty member at NYU's Tisch School for the Arts.

SUSAN HILFERTY (*Costume Design*) has designed more than 300 productions across the world. Directorial collaborators include Mantello, *Mayer,* MacAnuff, Lapine, Falls, Woodruff, Akalaitis, Garland Wright, Doug Wright, Lamos, Galati, Bobbie, Nelson, Ashley, Leon, Sher, Laurie Anderson, Hynes, Ellis, Edelstein, Eustis, Silverman, McDonald, Kushner and Fugard. Recent: *Annie* (Broadway), *Rigoletto* (Metropolitan Opera), Taylor Swift Speak/Now world tour, *The Road to Mecca, Wonderland, Spring Awakening* (Tony nomination). She chairs Graduate Design NYU/Tisch. Numerous awards include on Obie for Sustained Excellence and Tony, Drama Desk and Outer Critics Circle awards and Olivier nomination for *Wicked.* www.susanhilferty.com.

KEVIN ADAMS (*Lightning Designer*). Broadway: *American Idiot* (Tony Award), *Spring Awakening* (Tony Award), *Next to Normal* (Tony nom.), *Hair* (Tony nom.), *The 39 Steps* (Tony Award), *Everyday Rapture, Passing Strange, Man and Boy, Take Me Out.* Solo shows for John Leguizamo, Eve Ensler, Anna Deavere Smith, Eric Bogosian. Off-Broadway: *The Intelligent Homosexual's Guide...*, *Carrie, Rent, The Scottsboro Boys, Hedwig and the Angry Inch, Peter and Jerry, Some Men, Betty's Summer Vacation*, and Obie for Sustained Excellence. www.ambermylar.com.

STEVE CANYON KENNEDY (*Sound Design*) was the production engineer on such Broadway shows as Cats, *Starlight Express, Song & Dance, The Phantom of the Opera, Carrie* and *Aspects of Love.* Broadway sound design credits include *Hands on a Hardbody, Jesus Christ Superstar, Catch Me If You Can, Guys and Dolls, Mary Poppins, The Lion King, Jersey Boys* (Drama Desk Award), Billy Crystal's *700 Sundays, Hairspray, The Producers, Aida, Titanic, Big, How to Succeed in Business Without Really Trying, Carousel* and The Who's *Tommy* (Drama Desk Award).

MICHAEL KELLER (*Music Coordinator*). Broadway: *Kinky Boots, Motown the Musical, The Book of Mormon, Wicked, Mamma Mia!, The Lion King,* Upcoming: *First Date, Big Fish.* Tours: *Billy Elliot, Les Misérables, The Lion King, Memphis, Wicked.* Television: "Smash." Concert: Barbara Streisand (1994-2012). Pamela, Zachary, and Alexis make it all worthwhile.

TELSEY + COMPANY (*Casting*). Broadway/Tours: *Motown, Kinky Boots, Jekyll & Hyde, Annie, Newsies, Spider-Man Turn off the Dark, Rock of Ages, Wicked, Priscilla Queen of the Desert, Sister Act, Memphis, Million Dollar Quartet.* Off-Broadway: *The Last Five Years* (2nd Stage), Atlantic, MCC, Signature. Regional: La Jolla, Paper Mill. Film: *The Odd Life of Timothy Green, Friends with Kids, Joyful Noise, Margin Call, Sex and the City 1* and *2, I Love You Phillip Morris, Rachel Getting Married, Dan in Real Life, Across the Universe.* TV: "Smash," "The Big C." www.telseyandco.com

LINDA MARVEL (*Production Stage Manager*). Broadway: *Fela!, 33 Variations, The Little Dog Laughed, How to Succeed....* Off-Broadway: premieres of Fugard's *The Train Driver*, Ensler's *Emotional Creature*, Shepard's *The God of Hell* and Weller's *Beast*; Second Stage, Playwright's Horizons, Signature, NYTW, TFANA. Ms. Marvel is the production supervisor for *Seven*, being performed in Europe, Asia and the United States.

FORESIGHT THEATRICAL (*General Management*) is comprised of partners Alan Wasser, Allan Williams, Aaron Lustbader and Mark Shacket who oversee and supervise *The Phantom of the Opera* and *Spider-Man Turn Off the Dark* on Broadway, *Million Dollar Quartet* on tour and in Chicago and Las Vegas and executive produce *"I Love Lucy" Live on Stage.* Upcoming productions include *Kinky Boots, Tuck Everlasting, Charlie and the Chocolate Factory, Misery,* and *The Nutty Professor.*

TYPE A (*Marketing*) is an independent, full-service marketing company specializing in Broadway and national tours. Founded in 2008 by Anne Rippey, who continues to provide strategic supervision, Type A is led by Elyce Henkin and John McCoy who manage the campaigns for the current/upcoming roster, including Broadway's *Hands on a Hardbody, The Phantom of the Opera,* and *Tuck Everlasting* and the touring productions of *The Addams Family, American Idiot, Anything Goes, Flashdance the Musical, Million Dollar Quartet* and The Gershwins' *Porgy and Bess.* www.typeamktg.com

BROADWAY ACROSS AMERICA (*Producer*) is part of the Key Brand Entertainment family of companies which includes Broadway.com and is operated by British theatre producer John Gore (Owner and CEO). BAA is the foremost presenter of first-class touring productions across North America. Also a prolific producer, current/upcoming productions include *Hands on a Hardbody, Million Dollar Quartet, Pippin, The Testament of Mary, Tuck Everlasting, Big Fish, Little Miss Sunshine* and *The Blonde Streak*. Broadway.com is a premier theatre website for news, exclusive content and ticket sales. Visit BroadwayAcrossAmerica.com and Broadway.com.

BETH WILLIAMS (*Producer*) is currently CEO – Theater Division for Key Brand Entertainment, parent company of Broadway Across America. Producing credits include *How to Succeed in Business Without Really Trying*; *Million Dollar Quartet*; *On a Clear Day You Can See Forever*; *Promises, Promises*; *Grey Gardens*; *The Producers*; *Fosse*; and the upcoming *Tuck Everlasting, Little Miss Sunshine* and *The Blonde Streak*. Beth also worked as a conductor and/or pianist on *Les Misérables, Miss Saigon, The Phantom of the Opera* and *Dreamgirls*.

BARBARA WHITMAN (*Producer*). Broadway credits include *Red* (Tony® Award, Best Play), *Next to Normal, Hamlet* starring Jude Law, *33 Variations* starring Jane Fonda, *Mary Stuart, Legally Blonde: The Musical, The 25th Annual Putnam County Spelling Bee, Dirty Rotten Scoundrels* and *A Raisin in the Sun*. A native New Yorker, Barbara attended NYU's Gallatin School and received an MFA in Theatre Management and Producing from Columbia University. Her proudest productions are her sons, Daniel and Will.

LATITUDE LINK (*Producer*). Led by two-time Tony Award winning-producers, Ralph and Gail Bryan, Latitude Link is currently represented on Broadway by *Jersey Boys* (Tony® Award), *Hands on a Hardbody* and *Matilda*. Some past Broadway productions include *Memphis* (Tony® Award), *American Idiot, Jesus Christ Superstar, 33 Variations* and *The Farnsworth Invention*. Latitude Link shows have been enjoyed by more than 10 million people with 11 shows running on stages worldwide, including national and international productions of *Jersey Boys, Memphis* and *American Idiot*. www.latitudelink.com

DEDE HARRIS (*Producer*) has produced more than 35 Broadway, Off-Broadway and West End shows (winning six Tony Awards), including *Clybourne Park*; *One Man, Two Guvnors*; *War Horse*; *Jerusalem*; *9 to 5*; *The Norman Conquests*; *You're Welcome America*; *Speed-the-Plow*; *The Seagull*; *The Lieutenant of Inishmore*; *The History Boys*; *Dirty Rotten Scoundrels*; *A Raisin in* *the Sun; Golda's Balcony; Hairspray; The Crucible; Elaine Stritch: At Liberty; Noises Off; The Music Man.* Currently: *"I Love Lucy" Live on Stage.* In development: New musicals based on Diane Warren's music catalog and the book *The Wrecking Crew.* www.dedeharrisproductions.com

SHARON KARMAZIN (*Producer*). President, Good Karma Productions. Broadway: *Clybourne Park* (Tony® Award and Pulitzer Prize); *One Man, Two Guvnors; Ragtime* (Tony nomination); *Superior Donuts; The Seagull; You're Welcome America* with Will Ferrell (Tony nomination); *13; Dirty Rotten Scoundrels* (Tony nomination); *Steel Magnolias;* Mary Zimmerman's *Metamorphoses* (Drama Desk Award, Tony nomination); *Golda's Balcony.* Off-Broadway: *My Name Is Asher Lev, Altar Boyz* and others. Chicago: *"I Love Lucy" Live on Stage.* Board member: George Street Playhouse.

HOWARD AND JANET KAGAN (*Producer*). Broadway: 2012 Tony Award for The Gershwins' *Porgy and Bess*; also in 2012, *Bonnie & Clyde* and *The Anarchist.* Upcoming: *Pippin* (Broadway, spring 2013), *Tuck Everlasting* (Boston, summer 2013). Off-Broadway: the critically acclaimed *Not by Bread Alone.* Through their company Maxolev Productions, the Kagans look for entertaining commercial productions with atypical heroes, especially strong independent women. Mr. Kagan is on the board of the Off-Broadway theatre companies Ars Nova and The New Group.

JOHN AND CLAIRE CAUDWELL (*Producer*). John Caudwell is a high-profile, highly successful UK entrepreneur, philanthropist and supporter of many good causes, including his own charity Caudwell Children. Claire is John's long-term partner and mother to their son. Their previous Broadway productions include *Chaplin the Musical, Jesus Christ Superstar* and *Leap of Faith.*

ROUGH EDGED SOULS (*Producer*). **Deborah Taylor**: Broadway producer, check. Tony Award, check. Upcoming: *An American in Paris.* **Carl Moellenberg**: Four Tony Awards (*Spring Awakening, Hair, War Horse, Death of a Salesman*), 24 shows. **Wendy Federman**: Tony Award (*Hair*); 24 Broadway productions; three London; three national tours. **Sean Cercone**: Phan, Ironman and now Broadway producer. Hal and Snow, we did it!

JOYCE SCHWEICKERT (*Producer*). Executive producer/producer/actor for movies, including *Still Breathing, Twin Falls Idaho, Cherry Falls* and made-for-TV, "The Breed" and "Wild Iris." On Broadway, producer of *Dirty Rotten Scoundrels* and *The Pillowman*. Associated with Dede Harris Productions for *Hairspray* and revivals of *One Flew Over the Cuckoo's Nest, Noises Off* and others.

PAULA MARIE BLACK (*Producer*) is an owner/founder of the Four Graces wine brand in Oregon. *Hands on a Hardbody* marks her Broadway producing debut. Thank you to her children and grandsons for believing in the beauty of her dreams. From the first readings in New York all the way to this performance...she feels the joy!

BRUCE D. LONG (*Producer*). Involved in theatre, film and television as a director and producer for the last 20 years, Bruce is president and CEO of Eye Opening Entertainment. From documentary films to original series for PBS; currently in development is *By Grace*, a new musical about Grace Kelly. www.brucedlong.com

OFF THE AISLE PRODUCTIONS (*Producer*). Partners Orin Wolf and David F. Schwartz. Combined productions include-Broadway: *Orphans, Once* (Tony Award), *That Championship Season, A View From the Bridge*. Off-Broadway: *Not by Bread Alone, Groundswell, 25 Questions, Assume the Position* and *History of the Word*. Cofounders of OBB/Off-Broadway Booking.

BARBARA FREITAG (*Producer*). Barbara and her late husband Buddy formed B Square+4 Productions in 2004 with the mission of producing original musicals and plays. Credits: Lead producers of Memphis (2010 Tony for Best Musical), August: Osage County (Tony Award), The Drowsy Chaperone (five Tony Awards), Passing Strange (Tony nominations), November, The Mountaintop, Porgy and Bess and Nice Work If You Can Get It. Buddy and Barbara, a freelance writer, always shared a passion or theatre...She is continuing the love.

CHASE MISHKIN (*Producer*). Credits: *Dame Edna* (Tony recipient), "Sweeny Todd in Concert" (Emmy, PBS), plus more than a dozen Broadway shows including *Equus, Impressionism, Mary Stuart, Passing Strange, Little Women, Dirty*

Rotten Scoundrels, The Beauty Queen of Leenane, A Moon for the Misbegotten (Gabriel Byrne), *A Class Act, Dance of Death, Butley, Looped, Memphis* (Tony winner). Off-Broadway: over a dozen shows including *Gross Indecency, As Bees in Honey Drown.*

DAVID CARPENTER *(Associate Producer)* is the associate producer for Dede Harris Productions, overseeing creative development. Other producing credits include *"I Love Lucy" Live on Stage, But I'm a Cheerleader, Have a Nice Life* (NYMF). Previously he was the head of sales for DreamWorks Theatricals. Thank you to Dede, the amazing *Hardbody* family and Jacob.

JENNIFER COSTELLO *(Executive Producer)* has been with the company now known as Broadway Across America for more than 18 years. She began her career as the artistic director for an award-winning not-for-profit ensemble troupe. Deep love and gratitude to Beth Williams, her mentor, and Micah, Dylan and Finn, her lifeline.

LA JOLLA PLAYHOUSE *(Originally Produced By)*. The nationally acclaimed, Tony Award-winning La Jolla Playhouse is renowned for creating some of the most exciting, adventurous new work in the theatre. Twenty-four Playhouse productions have moved to Broadway, earning 35 Tonys, among them *Jersey Boys, Memphis, Big River, The Who's Tommy, I Am My Own Wife, Thoroughly Modern Millie, Chaplin, Peter and the Starcatcher.* Founded by Gregory Peck, Dorothy McGuire and Mel Ferrer, the Playhouse is led by artistic director Christopher Ashley and managing director Michael S. Rosenberg.

PRODUCTION PHOTOS

Photograph © Chad Batka

Keala Settle, Tony® Nominee for Best Performance by an Actress in a Featured Role (Musical). Keith Carradine, Tony® Nominee for Best Performance by an Actor in a Featured Role (Musical)

Photograph © Chad Batka

Original Broadway cast

Original Broadway cast

Photograph © Chad Batka

Performers Jay Armstrong Johnson and Allison Case

Photograph © Chad Batka

CHARACTERS

J.D. DREW – 60, a "good old boy" with pomaded gray hair and a high-wattage grin

KELLI MANGRUM – 22, a pretty brunette with steel ambition

BENNY PERKINS – mid-40s, with a lanky frame, weatherbeaten face, ingratiating grin and lots of homespun philosophy.

GREG WILHOTE – early 20s, a freckled white kid in a baseball cap

CHRIS ALVARO – well-built under his hoodie; a pair of aviator glasses conceal his eyes

RONALD McCOWAN – 35, is a good-natured African-American with a slight Louisiana accent

HEATHER STOVALL – 29, is a flirtatious blonde restaurant hostess

VIRGINIA DREW – J.D. Drew's wife, a one-time beauty settling into middle-age

MIKE FERRIS – sales manager, late 30s, boyishly handsome, and wears a cheap tie with a Nascar clip

CINDY BARNES – a former Miss Gregg County, still fond of pageant hair and pastels

JESUS PEÑA – a driven Mexican kid in his 20s

NORMA VALVERDE – is a stout Latina woman in tennis shoes and a floral applique t-shir

JANIS CURTIS – a tough old bird with sun-burnished skin and missing teeth

FRANK NUGENT – a die-hard good ole boy dressed in a Stetson

DON CURTIS – Janis' husband, wears a cardboard sign on his head that proclaims "I LOVE YOU JANIS, GO BABY GO!"

DR. STOKES – role can be played the actor who plays Don Curtis

SETTING

The Floyd King Nissan dealership, Longview, Texas.

MUSICAL NUMBERS

ACT ONE

"Human Drama Kind of Thing"
"If I Had this Truck"
"If She Don't Sleep"
"My Problem Right There"
"Alone With Me"
"Burn That Bridge"
"I'm Gone"
"Joy of the Lord"
"Stronger"
"Hunt With the Big Dogs"

ACT TWO

"Hands on a Hardbody"
"Born in Laredo"
"Alone With Me" (reprise)
"It's a Fix"
"Used to Be"
"It's a Fix" (reprise)
"God Answered My Prayers"
"Joy of the Lord" (reprise)
"Keep Your Hands On It"

PRODUCTION NOTES

THE TRUCK

The truck is a primary character in *Hands on a Hardbody*. Ideally, it is rendered realistically; it should have corporeality, heft and an alluring, shiny red finish.

For the New York production, we used a Nissan truck frame as the base, and augmented it with various fiberglass pieces. The engine was removed, and the weight stripped down to roughly 1400 pounds. Each corner rested on sixteen moving casters, right behind its four wheels. The actual wheels rested about half an inch off the ground, so the vehicle could roll in any direction with fluidity and grace.

Our truck had an operational horn, hood, tail lights and headlights, but it was in no way motorized; the actors maintained control of its movement at all times. For us, this was essential in our effort to be true to the material; a musical about real people should employ real elbow grease, real muscle, real sweat and no overtly artificial effects.

Despite the seemingly static nature of the piece–ten characters, all with their hands glued to the truck–we were able to create a vivid movement vocabulary; the cast quite literally danced with the truck. They danced around it, on top of it, while spinning it, often in continual motion. Sometimes, perverse limitations are a choreographer's best friend.

THE PASSAGE OF TIME

Our choreographer Sergio Trujillo collaborated with our lighting designer Kevin Adams to indicate the passage of time with accelerated light cues (like stop-motion images of the sun passing by overhead) and heightened movement (characters adopting dance-like postures to shield their eyes or wipe sweat from their brows.) These short, striking tableaus let us race forward through a story set in "real time" over ninety-one hours.

A NOTE ON ACTING

Despite their colorful eccentricities and regional turns of phrase, the characters in our story are inspired by very real people. They should not be played broadly, or with an implied "wink". Rather, they should be acted with integrity, with full regard for their ardent hopes, heart-breaking foibles and core decency.

ACT ONE

(A full-throttle guitar riff and a blinding flash and for an instant we see ten people gathered around a shiny new Nissan Hardbody truck, each with a hand planted on it. They've been standing for days, sans sleep, sans decent food. A young man paces furtively back and forth, running his hand up and down the bumper. A Latino kid does painstaking deep-knee bends. An older man sleeps standing-up. The image is ferocious and haunting; ten human beings in extremis. *It lingers long enough to sear itself into our consciousness, then one lone soul lets go of the truck and strides forward to address us as the image behind him fades.)*

BENNY. Stand here, simple as that. Stand here with your hand on the truck. Last one to take his hand off wins it. Sounds absurd, don't it? Some kind of sideshow. Maybe, maybe not.

(sunrise)

(We're in the dead-end land of discount stores; Walmart, Sam's Club and Best Buy. Among them, FLOYD KING NISSAN, LONGVIEW, TEXAS.)

(In the middle of the parking lot, that shiny, sexy little pick-up.)

*(SONG: **IT'S A HUMAN DRAMA THING**)*

BENNY. *(cont.)* *(spoken)*
EVERYTHING YOU THOUGHT YOU KNEW,
LEAVE THAT ALL BEHIND.
JUST KEEP ONE HAND ON THE TRUCK
AND TRY NOT TO LOSE YOUR MIND.

THIS IS NOT A CHILD'S GAME–
THIS IS NOT A GAME OF CHANCE–

BENNY. *(cont.) (sings)*

IT'S A SHARP HONED SKILL
IT'S A TEST OF WILL
IT'S KEEPIN' STILL
WHEN THE DEVIL TELLS YOU, "DANCE!"

(Sales manager **MIKE FERRIS** *opens the lot.)*

MIKE. Lot's open!

*(***CONTESTANTS*** storm onto the cement.)*

BENNY.

IT'S MORE THAN A CONTEST
IT'S MORE THAN DUMB LUCK
IT'S MORE THAN EXTRA CASH
IT IS MUCH MORE THAN A TRUCK!

SOMEONE'S GONNA CRY HERE
SOMEONE WILL GO INSANE
SOMEONE WILL BE LAUGHING
AT SOMEONE ELSE'S PAIN

BENNY.	**ALL.** *(except* **BENNY***)*
SOMEONE'S BOUND FOR GLORY	OOOOOOOH
THE REST ARE BOUND TO LOSE	
YOU'LL GET A HUNDRED DIFFERENT STORIES WITH A	OOOOOOOHH

ALL.

HUNDRED POINT OF VIEWS

BENNY.

EV'RY TEXAN NEEDS A RIDE
AND THIS TRUCK IS BONA FIDE
BUT ONLY ONE CAN GRAB THAT RING

ALL CONTESTANTS, DON, VIRGINIA.

AND GOD ALONE KNOWS WHAT HE'LL BRING

BENNY.

IT'S A HUMAN DRAMA KIND OF THING.

*(Disc Jockey **FRANK NUGENT** addresses the crowd:)*

FRANK. This is Frank Nugent, KYKX Kicks! 105.7 on your radio dial, coming to you live from the Hands on a Hardbody Contest here at Floyd King Nissan –

(He presses the dealership jingle.)

JINGLE.
FLOYD KING NISSAN
PICK UP AND GO!

FRANK. With me, sales manager Mike Ferris.

MIKE. Morning Frank!

FRANK. That is one slick-lookin', twenty-two thousand dollar truck!

MIKE. And we're giving it away!

FRANK. So anyone with the nerve–the tenacity–can drive away with the American Dream?

MIKE. Catchy ain't it? *Hands...*

(...and mimes placing them on a truck)

...on a Hardbody.

(gesturing toward the real truck)

That's a Hardbody.

BENNY, GREG, JESUS, RONALD, MIKE, FRANK, J.D., VIRGINIA.
SOME ARE ON VACATION
SOME ARE UNEMPLOYED
SOMEONE WILL DRIVE HOME ELATED
SOMEONE WILL WALK HOME DESTROYED

BENNY, HEATHER, NORMA, KELLI, JANIS, DON, MIKE, FRANK.
EVERYBODY'S BROKE HERE
TRYING TO MAKE ENDS MEET
PAY A DEBT BACK, HAD A SET BACK
GOT TO GET BACK ON OUR FEET

BENNY.
SO DON'T MAKE ANY JUDGMENTS
LET THE PLAYERS PLAY
LEAVE THE JUDGING TO THE JUDGE
WHO'LL JUDGE US ALL ON JUDGEMENT DAY!

BENNY, MIKE, FRANK, CINDY.
> BRING YOUR FAMILY COME ALONE
> GRAB A CORN DOG OR A CONE,
> GET YOURSELF A BLEACHER SEAT
> IN THE SHADE OUT OF THE HEAT
> FOR THIS HUMAN DRAMA KIND OF THING!

CONTESTANTS, DON & VIRGINIA.
> IF I WIN THIS TRUCK ALL MY TROUBLES ARE THROUGH
> JUST KEEP HOLDING ON
> THAT'S WHAT I'M GONNA DO
> SOMEONE'S GETTING LUCKY, NOW WHO WILL IT BE?
> IT'S ME! IT'S ME!

> *(**FRANK** interviews **CINDY BARNES**.)*

FRANK. Folks, here's Cindy Barnes, Public Relations here at Floyd King. Mornin', Ms. Barnes.

CINDY. Cindy.

FRANK. Today's contestants underwent a grueling screening process, did they not?

CINDY. We drew their names out of a hat. Business cards or beer coasters; it's all in the luck of the draw!

BENNY.
> I PUT MY NAME IN EARLY
> THERE'S TRICKS THAT YOU CAN DO

JESUS.
> I SPRINKLED MINE WITH COLA
> SO IT STICKS TO YOU LIKE GLUE

NORMA.
> I PUT MY FAITH IN JESUS
> HE ALWAYS SEES ME THROUGH

KELLI.
> I PUT MY NAME IN THIRTY-TWO TIMES, THIRTY-TWO TIMES!

JANIS.
> I GOT SIX MOUTHS TO FEED AND THESE ARE

CONTESTANTS, DON, VIRGINIA.
> TROUBLING TIMES!

HEATHER.
> I RODE MY BIKE HERE EVERY DAY!

J.D.

THAT PILE OF BILLS WON'T GO AWAY

RONALD.

I DRIVE A CAR AIN'T GOT NO BRAKES

CONTESTANTS, DON, VIRGINIA.

AND I'LL DO ANYTHING IT TAKES!

I NEVER WON NOTHING, I CAME ALL THE SAME.

I THOUGHT I WOULD DIE WHEN THEY CALLED OUT MY
NAME.

I PRAYED FOR A CHANGE TO COME YEAR AFTER YEAR,

IT'S HERE! IT'S HERE! IT'S HERE!

BENNY.	**CONTESTANTS, DON, VIRGINIA.**
LIKE THE GREAT ALI DID	MMMMMM
WHEN HE CHANGED HIS NAME FROM CASSIUS	OOOOOOHHHHH
EVERYBODY'S HOPING TO RISE	MMMMM
ONCE MORE FROM THE ASHES!	OOOHHH

NORMA.

O LORD–IT'S BEEN A REAL TOUGH YEAR

THANK YOU FOR THIS CHANCE RIGHT HERE

I'M SHAKING AND I'M SICK WITH FEAR, BUT

(add:)

JESUS, HEATHER, J.D., GREG, JANIS.

CAN I BEND YOUR EAR A MINUTE?

LOOK AT ALL THESE PEOPLE IN IT

ALL CONTESTANTS, DON, VIRGINIA.

JESUS I JUST GOT TO WIN

THIS TRUCK

THIS TRUCK

THIS TRUCK THIS TRUCK THIS TRUCK!

CINDY. The rules! One time, and one time only!

MIKE. Breaks are fifteen minutes once every six hours.

CINDY. You may not lean, squat or rest your legs.

MIKE. At no time may you remove your hand from the
truck.

CINDY. And that hand must be covered! We got cotton gloves here, courtesy of True Value Hardware–

(She waves a glove in the air.)

MIKE. No guns. No profanity.

CINDY. No alcohol or drugs.

ALL.

DON'T MAKE ANY JUDGMENTS
LET THE PLAYERS PLAY
LEAVE THE JUDGING TO THE JUDGE
WHO'LL JUDGE US ALL ON JUDGMENT DAY!

CONTESTANTS, DON, VIRGINIA.

THIS COULD BE MY TICKET OUT
LONG AS I JUST STICK IT OUT

ALL.

GET A GOOD SEAT IN THE STANDS

ALL. *(except* **CINDY***)*

FOR THE LAYING ON OF HANDS

*(***CINDY*** dispenses the gloves to the* **CONTESTANTS***.)*

CINDY. Gloves on!

(Eagerly, the **CONTESTANTS** *pull them on.)*

FRANK, BENNY, MIKE.

IT'S A HUMAN DRAMA KIND OF THING!

CONTESTANTS, DON, VIRGINIA.

I'LL STAND HERE FOR DAYS IN THE CROWDS AND THE HEAT

JANIS, J.D., NORMA, KELLI, GREG, HEATHER, CHRIS.

I AIN'T GIVIN' UP

KELLI, J.D., GREG, RONALD.

–I'M THE COWBOY TO BEAT!

ALL CONTESTANTS, DON, VIRGINIA. *(no* **BENNY***)*

SOMEONE'S GETTING LUCKY, NOW WHO WILL IT BE?
IT'S ME!
IT'S ME!

CHRIS.
> I'VE BEEN FEELING KIND
> OF LOW

>> **BENNY.**
>> IT'S A HUMAN DRAMA KIND
>> OF THING

GREG.
> NO WORK SINCE TWO
> YEARS AGO

>> **BENNY.**
>> IT'S A HUMAN DRAMA KIND
>> OF THING

JESUS.
> GUESS WHO'S DRIVING
> HOME THIS TRUCK?

ALL CONTESTANTS, DON.   **BENNY.**
> IT'S ME!   I'M LITTLE BUT I THINK
>   I'M BIG.
>   GONNA GET ALL RAMBO
>   ON THIS RIG!

CONTESTANTS, DON, VIRGINIA, CINDY.
> HERE'S REDEMPTION, NO TAX EXEMPTION
> BUT TRANSPORTATION AND INSPIRATION
> IF I JUST STAND AND I KEEP MY HAND ON THIS THING!

BENNY.
> IT'S A HUMAN DRAMA KIND OF THING!

CONTESTANTS, DON, VIRGINIA, CINDY.
> I'LL HONK MY HORN AGAIN, BE REBORN AGAIN
> BUSTED FLAT, NOW I'M UP TO BAT AND I SWING!

BENNY.
> THE WAY IT'S LOOKING HERE TO ME
> THE WINNER'S GONNA HAVE TO BE–BENNY!

CONTESTANTS, DON, VIRGINIA.
> A BODY'S GOT TO FEEL HIS WORTH
> REASON FOR HIS TIME ON EARTH
> GUESS WHOSE DRIVING
> HOME THIS TRUCK

NORMA, CHRIS, KELLI, JESUS, JANIS, DON.	HEATHER, VIRGINIA, BENNY, GREG, RONALD, J.D.
CAN I BEND YOUR EAR A MINUTE?	IT'S ME!

MIKE. Okay people, let's start this puppy!

NORMA, CHRIS, KELLI, JESUS, JANIS, DON.	HEATHER, VIRGINIA, BENNY, GREG, RONALD, J.D.
WON'T YOU LET ME DRIVE HOME IN IT!	ME!

CINDY. Ten seconds!

NORMA, CHRIS, KELLI, JESUS, JANIS, DON.	HEATHER, VIRGINIA, BENNY, GREG, RONALD, J.D.
JESUS, I JUST GOT TO WIN THIS	ME!

CINDY. Five!

ALL *but* **CINDY, MIKE, FRANK.**

TRUCK, THIS TRUCK, THIS TRUCK!

CINDY. Start the clock!

MIKE & **CINDY.**

HANDS ON!

(The **CONTESTANTS** *places their hands on the truck. They size one another up, warily. No one says a word for a long time.)*

(a vast, empty, gaping length of time)

(finally:)

KELLI. So this is it? Game on?

*(**RONALD** tosses a question out:)*

RONALD. How hot it 'sposed to get today?

JANIS. I heard a hundred and seven.

BENNY. With this asphalt, maybe hundred and twelve, hundred and fifteen.

RONALD. That's no problem for me; I love heat. You afraid of heat, you better not live in Texas! *Come on, heat, let's get it on! (a beat)* Now rain. I don't like no rain.

Thunder. Lightning. Storm comes, now that could be a problem right there.

(**HEATHER** *takes note of the strapping young* **CHRIS**:)

HEATHER. We can't take baths. Or showers. But I got six bottles of Mango Temptation body splash. I start to stink, I'll just slap on more of that.

(*behind his sunglasses,* **CHRIS** *is inscrutable;* **HEATHER** *deflates.*)

(*Meanwhile,* **JANIS** *draws a line in the sand with* **GREG**:)

JANIS. I stay on the fender; you stay on the gate. And we'll be fine.

GREG. Yes, ma'am.

(**GREG** *turns to* **KELLI** *for sympathy; why did he get stuck next to the cantankerous old broad?*)

Hey. Greg Wilhote.

KELLI. Kelli Mangrum. You see that guy there?

GREG. Benny Perkins?

KELLI. He already won two years ago! It's somebody else's turn.

GREG. He won't have the endurance; he must be forty years old.

(**BENNY** *admires the truck and says pointedly.*)

BENNY. Aztec red. She'll sure look nice next to the midnight blue one I already got.

KELLI. *(to GREG)* I'll drop on the floor and *die* before I let him win.

(**NORMA** *listens to her mp3 player.*)

NORMA. *(humming)*
I FEEL THE JOY
I FEEL THE JOY...

RONALD. She one smart lady; she brought herself some music.

JESUS. *Orale, música religiosa.*

RONALD. *(to* **NORMA**, *loudly)* That'll keep you awake, won't it?

NORMA. *(pulling an earphone aside)* Is it too loud? Some people think it's annoying.

RONALD. No! *Fortifyin'*. My daddy always told me, you live long enough, you gonna see problems only prayer can solve.

NORMA. Amen. My husband and I been praying for a truck, and I believe that this is what God wants me to do.

RONALD. Your husband? Where's he?

NORMA. Ramon? Over at unemployment.

RONALD. How come he send a lady to do a man's work?

NORMA. I think waiting there's worse than waiting here. Then he's gotta pick up our kids from school.

RONALD. You must be lonely without them kids.

NORMA. Oh, I'm not alone. I don't got people with me, but I got their prayers. Over at our church, they made a prayer chain for me. About a hundred families asking God to let me win. My brother in San Antonio, he started a chain at his church, too, so that's another six hundred or so. And my cousin in Waco, she goes to one of them Mega-Churches, they call 'em "Prayer Warriors" down there, must be two thousand. So every day, the Lord's got almost three thousand people prayin' "Give Norma that truck!" So I feel real blessed.

RONALD. Me, it's about glucose. When I was training back in high school, training for track, I used to eat an orange and a Snicker and that would carry me through the day.

*(***NORMA*** smiles at ***RONALD*** sweetly, and replaces her earphone. ***JESUS*** turns to ***HEATHER***:)*

JESUS. *Oye,* Miss. *A Toda Madre!* Nice truck, eh?

HEATHER. *(best hostess smile)* I'm so sorry; I don't *habla español.*

*(***JANIS*** glares at ***HEATHER***; she's not better than ***JESUS***!)*

JANIS. *(to JESUS) Buenos Dias.* You here to win today?

JESUS. Texas A&M, they have this school for veterinarians. They give me tuition, but the books, the housing, *mucho dinero.* I sell this truck, I go. *(a beat)* You?

JANIS. Got six reasons I'm here: Tolbert, Anne Marie, John Earl, John Franklin, John David and our youngest, Bev-Sue. *(with gravity)* And believe you me, I finish whatever I start.

BENNY. *(to KELLI)* Pretty girl like you, what you need with a truck?

KELLI. *(snapping back)* You won before, what you need with two?

BENNY. *(maintaining his cool)* No disrespect, little lady, but if anybody's gonna beat me…*if that person's truly out there…*it'd have to be someone with the conditioning. Somebody, say, fresh outta the Marine Corps. My son was a Marine. *(a beat)* I'll admit, that person could possibly beat me.

(CHRIS *strips off his hoodie to reveal a camouflage t-shirt, emblazoned with USMC.*)

(BENNY *swallows hard.* KELLI *and* GREG *stifle giggles. Even* J.D. *breaks into a grin.*)

(*Over in the pit, an enthusiastic* DON *turns to* VIRGINIA.)

DON. You somebody's pit crew?

VIRGINIA. I guess I am.

DON. See that lady there? That's my wife, Janis. You tell her she can't do something, she's gonna do it. I told her, "Baby, you can't win," just to give her an edge. You got a horse in this race?

VIRGINIA. He's got no business being here. Six months ago, the man was strung up in a hospital in traction.

DON. No joke?

VIRGINIA. Doc says he shouldn't even be climbing stairs.

(*Back at the truck,* RONALD *effuses to* NORMA:)

RONALD. –a car's gonna git you there, but a truck? *A truck change your life.* I win, I start my own landscape business. "McCowan and Sons." *(with a wink)* First I get the truck, then I get to work on the sons.

KELLI. *(to GREG)* You ever owned a truck before?

GREG. I wish.

KELLI. What you driving now?

GREG. *(blushing)* It don't matter…

BENNY. I'd like to know too, son. We're all curious, ain't we?

HEATHER. Kinda, yeah.

BENNY. What is it? Corvette? Mustang, maybe? Dual quads and a six pack–

GREG. Come on, dawg–

BENNY. Go ahead, Junior. Impress the lady.

GREG. *(to KELLI, an agonized whisper)* Promise you won't laugh?

(KELLI nods solemnly.)

A VW Bug. My Mama's.

(KELLI can't help cracking a smile)

HEATHER. Oh, I love those! My sorority sister had one! Candy white with a daisy decal on the hood–!

J.D. Son, this town, you're lucky you're still alive.

GREG. *(to KELLI)* I get this new truck, I oughtta fit right in.

*(SONG: **IF I HAD THIS TRUCK**)*

J.D.
A TRUCK TO A TEXAN
IS JUST LIKE HIS HAT

BENNY.
YOU DON'T FEEL COMPLETE
IF YOU AIN'T GOT THAT

RONALD.
A TRUCK IS A MARKER
A PART OF THE PLAN

THAT SAYS YOU'RE GROWN UP
THAT SAYS YOU'RE A MAN

GREG.

IF YOU LIVE IN THE NORTH, YOU CAN DRIVE A SEDAN

JESUS.

BUT IF YOU LIVE IN TEXAS
AND YOU AIN'T GOT NO TRUCK
BUDDY YOU'RE STUCK

ALL MALE CONTESTANTS, DON.

BUDDY YOU'RE STUCK.
IF I HAD THIS TRUCK
I'D HAVE A PIECE OF THE PIE
IF I HAD THIS TRUCK
AND A DROP OF GOOD LUCK
I MIGHT GET BY

HEATHER.

DADDY WISHED HE'D HAD A BOY
HE RAISED ME TO BE TOUGH
HE AND MAMA ALWAYS FOUGHT
AND WHEN HE'D HAD ENOUGH
HE'D GRAB HIS HAT AND COAT
AND THOUGH I WAS ONLY FIVE
HE'D SAY COME WITH ME LITTLE GIRL
I'M GONNA TEACH YOU HOW TO DRIVE
AND HE'D LET THE ENGINE WARM UP
AND HE'D SAY 'YOUR COACH AWAITS'
AND HE'D LIFT ME IN THAT DUSTY TRUCK
WITH THE RUSTY LICENSE PLATES.
THERE WAS NO HEAT IN THE CAB
AND FOUR DIFFERENT KIND OF WHEELS
AND I THOUGHT, MAN
NOW I KNOW HOW CINDERELLA FEELS

IF I HAD THIS TRUCK
I'D BE OKAY ON MY OWN
NO MORE RIDING MY BIKE
COME AND GO AS I LIKE
JUST ME ALONE

KELLI.
>IF I HAD THIS TRUCK
>MAN THAT WOULD BE HOT
>I'D FLIP FOLKS THE BIRD
>AS I PEEL OUT THE LOT

NORMA.
>WHEN I WIN THIS TRUCK
>I'LL GIVE THANKS TO THE LORD
>TILL THE DAY THAT I GO
>TO MY PROPER REWARD

JANIS.
>IF YOU LIVE IN THE SOUTH
>YOU CAN DRIVE AN ACCORD

NORMA.
>BUT IF YOU LIVE IN TEXAS
>AND YOU AIN'T GOT NO TRUCK
>HONEY YOU'RE STUCK

ALL WOMEN CONTESTANTS.
>HONEY YOU'RE STUCK

ALL CONTESTANTS, DON.
>IF I HAD THIS TRUCK
>I'D HAVE A PIECE OF THE PIE

KELLI, NORMA, GREG, BENNY, HEATHER, JANIS, J.D., RONALD.	**DON.**
IF I HAD THIS TRUCK	AAAAAHHH

KELLI, NORMA, GREG, CHRIS, HEATHER, JANIS, DON, J.D., JESUS.	**BENNY, RONALD.**
I'D HOLD MY HEAD UP HIGH	HEAD UP HIGH

BENNY.
>NO, I WON'T LEAVE 'TIL I WIN

GREG.
>AND MY LIFE CAN BEGIN

HEATHER.
>SWEET JESUS, I HATE MY SCHWINN

NORMA.
>I KNOW TO COVET'S A SIN

ALL.

> BUT PICTURE ME DRIVING IN
>
> ...MY BRAND NEW TRUCK!
> MY BRAND NEW TRUCK.

RONALD.

> CAR DON'T MAKE MONEY
> TRUCK–MAKE MONEY.
>
> (**FRANK** *corners* **CINDY.**)

FRANK. Crowd just keeps growing, Cindy. I've seen license plates from Louisiana and Arkansas. What can foreign visitors expect to find here in Longview?

> (**CINDY** *does her damnedest to be a worthy community booster:*)

CINDY. Longview is a commercial hub here in East Texas, right near the Piney Woods. Originally, the town was called Earpville. But our founders, Mr. Methvin and Mr. Whaley, stood atop a hill one day and remarked to one another, "What a *long view.*" Hence, our name today. Famous residents include Karen Silkwood, because they made a movie about her, and... *(turning bright red)* ...Matthew McConaughey; he was *The Sexiest Man Alive* in the year 2005, and don't say I told you so, but here at *Floyd King Nissan*, we got that *People Magazine* cover hanging up in the ladies' lounge.

FRANK. You hear that, ladies?

CINDY. *(with a heavy heart)* Of course, foreclosures in Gregg county are running about a hundred a month and what with that toxic spill down at Lake Cherokee–

> (**FRANK** *whispers in* **CINDY**'s *ear*)

CINDY. *(taking* **FRANK**'s *save)* Oh, but we're still a shopper's paradise! Not one but three Walmart Super Centers–!

> *(the piercing sound of a whistle)*

MIKE. All right, people, this is fifteen! Take fifteen!

> *(The* **CONTESTANTS** *let go, shaking out their hands and feet. They disperse to their "pit stations," lawn chairs and picnic baskets.)*

(**J.D.** *heads toward* **VIRGINIA,** *a crick in his step.*)

VIRGINIA. What's a matter, sweetie? It giving you pain already?

J.D. Hush up. You want the whole world to know? I'm the oldest one here; that's bad enough.

VIRGINIA. Baby, calm down.

J.D. Mexican kid; he's strong. And that girl on the tailgate, she's hell-bent 'n ready–

VIRGINIA. We gotta keep this leg elevated much as we can–

(She places a cooler so he can use it as a stool, and tries raising his leg on top of it. He resists.)

J.D. Damn it! This ain't the ICU.

VIRGINIA. You know what happens when you stand too long.

J.D. Only one thing giving me a pain right now.

VIRGINIA. *(stung)* What in God's name do we need with a truck?

J.D. *What do we need with a truck?* We got no money–

VIRGINIA. Well, if you'd let me take that job at the Walmart–

J.D. For a hundred and eighty-six dollars in take-home? And no benefits?

VIRGINIA. What's comin' in now, baby? Answer me that.

J.D. *Why the hell you think I'm here?*

VIRGINIA. You might as well drive to Shreveport, play the casinos. A blackjack table, at least you'd be sittin' down.

*(**VIRGINIA** tends to his leg, rolling up his trousers to tighten the brace on it.)*

You're supposed to *stay off this,* so the bones can fuse. All those months flat on your back, woozy from the meds, talking like a crazy person… *(affectionately)* …I can't do it again, never mind you. Here, baby, here's your juice box.

*(She hands **J.D.** some apple juice, then feels his forehead.)*

Oh, you're on fire.

(She takes out a pink washcloth with an embroidered edge, wets it with bottled water and drapes it over his head.)

VIRGINIA. *(cont.)* You sit pretty. I'm goin' to the K Mart, get you more sun-screen.

*(**BENNY** notices **J.D.**, looking miserable with the juice box in hand and the rag on his head. He approaches. Distraught, **J.D.** pulls out a pack of cigarettes, and slides one out.)*

BENNY. Nice hat.

*(**J.D.** grabs the cloth off his head and throws it onto the ground. **BENNY** offers him a light.)*

Little lady's got you wrapped, tight.

J.D. She's just worried 'bout me.

BENNY. How come?

J.D. I fell off a rig.

BENNY. Sun Petroleum?

J.D. Lone Star Fuel.

BENNY. What they do for ya?

J.D. Fired me so I lost my pension, then sent me a basket of grapefruit. *(a mordant sigh)* Got more pins in me than a bowling alley.

BENNY. No offense, Old Timer, but I'll be surprised if you're still here come nightfall.

*(**J.D.** gives **BENNY** the once-over then observes drily.)*

J.D. You're past the draft, too, looks like.

*(**BENNY** nods toward **KELLI.**)*

BENNY. Goddamn kids. Half of 'em don't even look old enough to drive. *(bristling) I put my name in, same as anybody. Nothing and nobody says I can't.*

J.D. Amen, friend. You got every right.

BENNY. *(defensively flaring)* What you say?

J.D. *(admiringly)* They're scared, that's all. You're a proven entity.

(**BENNY**'s *found a friend. He grins and extends his hand.*)

BENNY. Benny Perkins.

J.D. J.D. Drew. Where's your better half?

BENNY. My wife, she couldn't make it.

J.D. Why not?

BENNY. That truck I won two years ago? Last February, she loaded it up with her suitcases and her Mary Kay and she drove off. I been driving a '96 Impala ever since. *(a beat)* Old dogs like us, we got to stick together.

J.D. You're the man with the know-how. The *experience.*

BENNY. I am indeed.

J.D. Reckon I could use a little of what you got.

BENNY. You askin'?

J.D. You givin'?

BENNY. You ever study tae kwon do with a Master?

J.D. Huh?

BENNY. You willing to pledge yourself to me the way a young Korean warrior pledges himself to his *Saseong?*

J.D. His who?

BENNY. The way you pledge yourself to your Sherpa, 'fore you climb Everest? "I will eat your *shyakpa.* I will follow in the footsteps of your sacred yak."

(**J.D.** *balks at* **BENNY.**)

J.D. You're talkin' crazy now.

BENNY. Crazy? I'll tell you what's crazy. *Vanity.* Vanity that says, "I can get through this alone." Oh, you're fine six hours in, but by day three, you're gonna want somebody in the foxhole with you. Who's it gonna be? V.W. Bug Boy? Church Lady? Little missus on the sidelines, givin' you juice boxes and sorrowful looks?

(**J.D.** *'s cheeks turn red.*)

BENNY. Me, I'd want the one man who could be my brother.

(**BENNY** *spits in his palm, then holds it out for* **J.D.** *to shake*)

What do you say?

(*A final moment of consideration, and* **J.D.** *takes* **BENNY**'s *proffered hand.*)

J.D. All right, my brother.

BENNY. Now, I'm gonna give you a code word. I'll use this word when my mind starts to free fall. That gives you permission to punch me, slap me, kick me–whatever it takes.

J.D. Okay then.

BENNY. That word is…"Cuervo." Ready? Set. Go. *Cuervo!*

(**J.D.** *slaps him*)

Harder. *Cuervo!*

(**J.D.** *gives him a second, more vigorous slap.*)

Ow.

J.D. You'll do the same for me?

BENNY. Absolutely.

(**BENNY** *offers* **J.D.** *a fist bump*)

You and me, final two?

J.D. Final two.

(*their deal is sealed*)

(**CINDY** *blows her whistle: The* **CONTESTANTS** *reassemble and pull their gloves on.*)

CINDY. Five…four…three…two…one…hands on!

(*And they place their hands back on the truck. There's a commotion in the pit:*)

DON. Getting sleepy, ain't you baby? Your head's gettin' heavy–?

JANIS. I'm wide awake, fool.

DON. Your knees about to buckle, ain't they?

JANIS. *Hush! My knees is fine–*

(**GREG** *can't help himself; even crusty old* **JANIS** *doesn't deserve this treatment.*)

GREG. Whoa, Mister, what you doin'?

DON. *(beaming)* Reverse psychology. Works like a charm.

(**JANIS** *enthusiastically concurs, offering a cheerful nod:*)

JANIS. Yup.

(**FRANK** *intercedes.*)

FRANK. You, sir! Yes you! Sounds like you've got someone special in the contest today.

DON. My name is Don Curtis, and I'm here to support my wife Janis.

(*SONG: **IF SHE DON'T SLEEP**)*

(*sings*)

YOU TRY TO FIND A JOB THAT PAYS
WAIT AROUND FOR BETTER DAYS
LIFE CAN WEAR YOU DOWN
AND THAT'S A FACT
BUT WE ALWAYS COME UP FIGHTIN'
AND LIFE IS PLAIN EXCITIN'
CAUSE HER AND ME
WE GOT THIS LITTLE PACT.
IF SHE DON'T SLEEP, THEN I DON'T SLEEP

JANIS.

IF HE DON'T EAT, THEN I DON'T EAT

DON.

AND LIFE IS SWEET, WITH SIX KIDS ALMOST GROWN

JANIS.

IT'S TRUE WE MAY NOT HAVE A LOT

DON.

IF I GOT SQUAT, THEN SHE GOT SQUAT

BOTH.

BUT WE DON'T HAVE TO GO THROUGH IT ALONE.

DON.

IF YOU WRITE HER OFF THEN YOU'LL REGRET IT
YOU DON'T SEE THE WOMAN THAT I SEE

SHE'S STRONGER THAN MOST PEOPLE GIVE HER CREDIT
PLUS SHE'S GOT HER SECRET WEAPON–ME

(spoken)

I told her, "Janis, you got to get used to long hours in the heat. You been sittin' under the air conditioner." She's spoiled on accounta I got a twenty-ton unit on my home.

FRANK. You have a what?

DON. Most people's is three tons at the most. But me? I got a twenty.

JANIS & DON.

20 TONS OF AIR
THE BIGGEST THING YOU EVER SEEN!

DON.

IT USED TO COOL A KMART
THAT WENT BUST IN ABILENE

JANIS & DON.

IT BRINGS OUR HOUSE TO TWELVE BELOW
AND YOU CAN SEE YOUR BREATH!

JANIS.

AND WE FOUND OUT PRETTY QUICKLY
IT WILL FREEZE A PET TO DEATH.

DON.

I COULDN'T PASS THE UNIT UP
IT WAS TOO GOOD A BUY
BUT UNLESS SHE GOT USED TO THIS HEAT
I KNEW JANIS WOULD DIE.

JANIS.

HE KNEW THAT I WOULD DIE.

DON.

EVERY TIME SHE STEPPED OUTSIDE
SHE GOT RED AS A TURNIP
SO I HAD TO TURN THE UNIT OFF
SO SHE WOULDN'T BURN UP!

DON.   **JANIS.**

IF SHE AIN'T COOL

                                    IF HE AIN'T COOL

THEN I AIN'T COOL

                   THEN I AIN'T COOL

BOTH.

YOU'D BE A FOOL TO DO THIS ON YOUR OWN

DON.

IF SHE DON'T CRY, THEN I DON'T CRY

LONG AS SHE'S HAPPY, SO AM I

AND SHE DON'T HAVE TO GO THROUGH THIS ALONE

BOTH.

OH, WE DON'T HAVE TO GO THROUGH THIS ALONE.

*(**DON** winks affectionately at his wife and recedes to the pit.)*

*(From inside the climate-controlled, fluorescent office, **MIKE** surveys the scene:)*

MIKE. So far, not a single man down.

CINDY. That Mangrum girl's got the edge. Eatin' bananas for potassium. And look, she's got sneakers with those big waffle bottoms.

MIKE. Longer we milk this thing, the more foot traffic.

CINDY. We're gettin' run-off from the interstate, thanks to that new Sam's Club. And did you see our promo last night on KLTV–

MIKE. Hell yes.

*(**MIKE** picks up his sunglasses to use as a mirror.)*

That teeth bleach paid off.

CINDY. They picked it up and ran it as far away as Houston–

MIKE. *(gleeful)* Hee-hee! *(then derisively)* Dan Frankel in Tennessee, he says to me, "What the hell kinda Big Ass order is this? Last six months, you ain't made quota–"

CINDY. He is such a donkey dick, I swear–

MIKE. –and I told him, "You don't understand, Dan, my man. Last summer, Hands on a Hardbody, I moved twelve Maximas, eight Pathfinders, and six Altima Coupes. You tell me one dealership in East Texas that had a better July. Now I want the same units this year."

CINDY. We fall behind but we sure as hell catch up–

MIKE. "We'll be watching," he says to me, "from Tennessee all the way to Tokyo. We'll be watching."

(self-satisfied) "You'll be watching," I tell him, "to see how it's done."

(musing to himself) You give 'em a circus, they buy souvenirs.

CINDY. I saw Mrs. Ferris at the Kroger. She said you was lookin' at Tuscan marble for your new kitchen.

MIKE. Nothing wrong with wanting nice things. That's what makes the world spin. Hell, that's patriotism.

CINDY. I'll see you at sun up!

*(**CINDY** makes for the door and exits.)*

(Time passes. Light darkens to night; the hum of floodlights, the chirping of cicadas.)

*(**MIKE** steps onto the lot, bullhorn in hand:)*

MIKE. *Buenos noches,* people!

(He retreats inside.)

RONALD. Mosquitos out fierce tonight. I don't mind that, I can handle that. But chiggers? Chiggers could be a problem right there.

JESUS. Somebody's gonna fall soon.

JANIS. Nobody wants to be the first one.

HEATHER. I got me some Baby Wipes, fresh me right up.

JANIS. First one falls off, they'll start dropping like flies.

*(**BENNY** says to **J.D.** sotto voce:)*

BENNY. One thing you don't want? That's goin' numb. When you go numb, you'd better start worrying.

J.D. You got a strategy for that?

BENNY. No strategy. You go numb, you're goin' down.

*(A nauseous **RONALD** turns to **NORMA,** clutching his stomach:)*

RONALD. What number Snicker bar was that?

NORMA. Fifteen, maybe?

RONALD. Man, that last one didn't go down so good. This clock-work got me all messed up. We been here sixteen hours?

BENNY. *(to* **J.D.***)* His trouble? He's got no plan.

RONALD. What'd he just say?

BENNY. *(to* **RONALD***)* I said, *you didn't think it through.* You underestimated the effort here today, and you did not prepare.

RONALD. Hey. Hey, hey. *(staring* **BENNY** *down)* You from Longview? I'm from Marshall. Longview got three post offices; Marshall got one. Longview got a twelve story building; Marshall got none. But that don't matter *today*. I'm goin' the distance here *today*.

KELLI. You tell him, Ronald!

HEATHER. Whoo-hoo! Ronnie! Whoo!

RONALD. Today, I get me a page in the history books!

JANIS. That's right!

RONALD. Plan? Oh, I got a plan!

KELLI. 'Course you do!

*(SONG: **MY PROBLEM RIGHT THERE**)*

RONALD. I got no problems, except for this one problem.

BENNY. Just one, huh?

RONALD. Yeah, just the one.

KELLI. You tell him, Ronnie!

RONALD. *(sings)*

> I DIDN'T GET NO SLEEP LAST NIGHT
> I WAS THINKING ABOUT TODAY
> TRY TO KEEP THINGS SIMPLE
> BUT MY BRAIN GETS IN THE WAY.
>
> I SAID, 'YOU NEED TO REST NOW'
> BUT MY BIG HEAD DON'T CARE
> NOW I CAN SEE, THAT THAT'S GONNA BE
> MY PROBLEM RIGHT THERE.

MY PROBLEM RIGHT THERE
MY PROBLEM RIGHT THERE
MY POWERFUL MIND
THAT'S MY PROBLEM RIGHT THERE

I GOT NO OTHER PROBLEMS
OF WHICH I'M AWARE
I'M JUST TOO DAMN SMART

RONALD, KELLI, HEATHER, NORMA.

THAT'S MY/HIS PROBLEM RIGHT THERE.

*(**RONALD**'s cell phone rings.)*

Hello? Oh, hey Peaches...no, no, I'm YOUR boo, Baby. Don't go around believing all the tattoos you read. Look, I'm in the middle of something; I'll check you later.

RONALD.	**GIRLS.**
THAT'S PEACHES FROM TULSA	
	OOOO-OOOOO
CALLING AGAIN	
	CALLED YOU UP
THERE ONCE WAS A TIME I WENT HOME WITH HER FRIEND	
	NO NO
NOW THEY BOTH SAY THEY'RE COMING	
	UH OH!
TO BE BY MY SIDE,	
AIN'T NO ROOM IN THIS TRUCK	AIN'T NO ROOM
TO TAKE THREE FOR A RIDE!	
	BEEP BEEP!
MY PROBLEM RIGHT THERE	HIS PROBLEM,
MY PROBLEM RIGHT THERE	HIS PROBLEM RIGHT THERE. OOH

THESE WOMEN ROUND HERE	
ARE MY PROBLEM RIGHT THERE	
I COULD HANDLE THEM ALL	OOOOOOOOHHHH
BUT THEY DON'T LIKE TO SHARE	OOOOHHHH YA YA!
I GOT TOO MUCH LOVE!	
THAT'S MY PROBLEM	THAT'S HIS PROBLEM
RIGHT THERE.	THAT'S HIS PROBLEM RIGHT THERE.

RONALD. *(to* **GREG***)* You know what I'm talking about boy!

GIRLS.

LIKE YOUR DAYS RUNNING TRACK
YOU WON'T QUIT TIL YOU'VE WON

RONALD.   **GIRLS.**

NO WAY!	
AND I'LL RUN THROUGH THE PAIN	
AND THAT FIERCE PRAIRIE SUN	
BUT IF IT STARTS TO RAIN	OOOOOOOHHHH
RONALD OUT! I DON'T CARE!	

(There's a crack of thunder; **RONALD** *ducks.)*

RONALD.

NOW *THAT'S* GONNA BE MY PROBLEM RIGHT THERE!

GIRLS.

HIS PROBLEM RIGHT THERE.
THAT'S HIS PROBLEM RIGHT THERE.
BRAINS, WOMEN AND RAIN
ARE HIS PROBLEM RIGHT THERE

RONALD.

AND JUST LOOK WHAT THIS CAP
HAS DONE DONE TO MY HAIR!

BENNY.

LOOKS LIKE YOU'VE GOT
ONE MORE PROBLEM RIGHT THERE.

RONALD. Ooh, Lord!

....MAN THE HEAT AND THE SWEET
FROM MY FIFTEENTH SNICKER
ARE WORKING ON ME
LIKE MY DADDY'S CORN LIQUOR
AND THE CORNS ON MY FEET
GETTIN' SWEATY AND SLICKER
FEEL THE CANDY REPEAT
AND IT MAKES ME FEEL SICKER

HEATHER, NORMA & KELLI.

BUT YOU'VE GOT NO OTHER PROBLEMS
OF WHICH YOU'RE AWARE

RONALD.

EXCEPT I THINK I'M GONNA LOSE
AND I DON'T REALLY CARE.

(The sugar intake, heatstroke and sour tummy get the better of **RONALD**. *His hand slides off the truck. He stares at it, marveling.)*

LOOKY HERE! I'M LETTING GO
AND I'M HOLDING ON TO AIR.

(The **OTHERS** *gasp.)*

YES SIREE
THAT'LL HAVE TO BE
THAT'LL HAVE TO BE
MY BIGGEST PROBLEM–

HEATHER, KELLI, NORMA.

NO!

RONALD

RIGHT–

HEATHER, KELLI, NORMA.

NO!

RONALD.	HEATHER, KELLI, NORMA.
–THERE.	NO, NO RONALD! DON'T GO!

BENNY. First man down!

*(**FRANK** cues the jingle, a tradition whenever a contestant drops off the truck.)*

JINGLE.
FLOYD KING NISSAN
PICK UP AND GO!

FRANK. Mr. Ronald McCowan. Always hurts to be the first.

BENNY. Yes! Ya feel it? Breathe it in, people!

*(**MIKE** pats **RONALD**'s cheeks until he comes back to consciousness.)*

RONALD. What jus' happened? Lord, don't tell me. It's over. Am I over?

*(**RONALD** is bewildered, like a wild animal that's been sedated. **MIKE** pulls him up and guides him off the lot.)*

*(**BENNY** mocks his demise.)*

BENNY.
KILLED BY CANDY
KILLED BY CANDY.
OH LORD, KILLED BY CANDY.
*(to **J.D.**)* Big surprise, he's first to go.

NORMA. *(leaping to **RONALD**'s defense)* What's that supposed to mean?

BENNY. Wasn't talking to you.

JANIS. Low blood sugar; that's what done it.

BENNY. *(all innocence now)* Yes, mam, that's all I meant. *(to **J.D.** with indignation)* What she think I was saying?

NORMA. *Shame on you. (with empathy for **RONALD**)* He's already down. He's lost. He's a good man, and he's not coming back.

*(**BENNY** imparts more sotto voce wisdom to **J.D.**)*

BENNY. She won't last. Too soft. *(nodding toward* **JESUS***)* Now Tex Mex over there, he could be the man to beat. Wants it somethin' fierce. Fit six of his buddies in the back, no one's the wiser.

JANIS. *(to* **JESUS***)* Pay him no mind; he's a low-down dog.

JESUS. Please, *Senora.* Don't insult the dog.

BENNY. *(still confidentially to* **J.D.***)* "If you know your enemy and know yourself, your victory will not stand in doubt." Fella named Sun Tzu. *The Art of War.*

MIKE. *(blows his whistle)* Break time, people! Shake 'em and stretch 'em!

(The **CONTESTANTS** *disperse.* **VIRGINIA** *calls to* **J.D.***)*

VIRGINIA. Baby, you want your pain pills?

J.D. No'm.

(J.D and **BENNY** *lock eyes for a beat.)*

VIRGINIA. I got extras, right here in my bag. Got your anti-inflammatories, too, and that calcium drink you like–

J.D. *(sharply)* Quit! Just QUIT!

*(***VIRGINIA***'s taken aback, but* **J.D.** *keeps right on going:)*

How'm I 'sposed to get back on my feet if you won't let me? Hovering over me the way you do, fussing all the time, pushing and poking, treating me like an overgrown child–*I'm telling you, I can't take it–*

VIRGINIA. *(wounded but covering it)* Well alright.

J.D. That…ah…that's not what I meant.

VIRGINIA. Isn't it?

*(SONG: **ALONE WITH ME**)*

(sings)

WHEN I WAS SEVENTEEN AND YOU WERE TWENTY-THREE,
YOU COULDN'T WAIT TO BE ALONE WITH ME.
WE SHARED A PRIVATE LITTLE WORLD ALL OUR OWN
THEN THE KIDS CAME–NO PRIVACY
THE JOB TOOK YOU AWAY FROM ME

STILL, WE'D NEVER MISS
OUR GOODNIGHT KISS ON THE PHONE.

REMEMBER HOW WE'D WHISPER DEAR
AND DREAM ABOUT THE DAY
WHEN IT WOULD BE THE TWO OF US
AND YOU'D BE HOME TO STAY?
NOW YOU JUST WANT TO WIN THIS TRUCK
SO YOU CAN DRIVE AWAY
TO HUNT WITH THE BOYS
AND MAKE YOU FEEL FREE
YOU'D DO ANYTHING
TO KEEP FROM BEING ALONE WITH ME.

VIRGINIA.	J.D.
YOU'RE TIRED OF THE GROWING BILLS	I'M JUST TIRED
THE SIDE EFFECTS FROM THE LITTLE PILLS	ALL THE TIME
AND THE HOSPITALS WHERE	

BOTH.

THEY JUST WON'T LET YOU/ME BE.

VIRGINIA.

I THOUGHT THAT YOU'D BE HAPPY NOW
HOME WITH THE ONE YOU LOVE
BUT IT TURNS OUT I'M ONE MORE THING
YOU'VE GOTTEN TIRED OF
I TRY TO TALK,

J.D.

I DON'T WANT TO TALK

VIRGINIA.

YOU TURN UP THE TV.

J.D.

JUST LET ME BE

VIRGINIA.

YOU USED TO LIKE BEING–

J.D.

I CAN'T STAND BEING–

BOTH.
> ALONE WITH ME.

VIRGINIA.
> AFTER THIRTY YEARS,
> YOU GUESS SOME LOVE WILL WEAR AWAY
> THE SAME FACE ON YOUR PILLOW
> STARING AT YOU EVERY DAY

BOTH.
> AFRAID THAT YOU'LL DISCOVER
> YOU HAVE NOTHING LEFT TO SAY.

VIRGINIA.
> I WISH I KNEW
> WHAT I COULD DO
> TO MAKE MYSELF ENOUGH FOR YOU
> THE WAY THAT YOU'RE ENOUGH FOR ME.

J.D. *(regretfully)* Aw, Ginny.

VIRGINIA.
> BUT I CAN'T WATCH YOU KILL YOURSELF
> IT'S KILLING ME
> YOU'D DO ANYTHING
> TO KEEP FROM BEING ALONE WITH ME.

> *(**VIRGINIA** exits. **J.D.** looks after her, discomfitted.)*

> *(Meanwhile, **MIKE** approaches **HEATHER**, who's milling about in hopes of using the restroom on her break.)*

MIKE. That's a mighty long line for the Port-A-Potty.

HEATHER. I'll say.

MIKE. You wanna use the executive washroom? It's nice and cool in there.

HEATHER. Am I allowed–?

MIKE. *(under his breath)* What you waitin' for, an engraved invitation?

> *(**HEATHER** glances furtively about, then follows **MIKE** into the office.)*

> *(Once safely inside, they drop all pretense. These two aren't what you'd call strangers. In fact, they shoot sparks.)*

MIKE. *(cont.)* So, pretty lady, you in or you out?

HEATHER. I don't know–

MIKE. Honey, we are down to the wire–

HEATHER. I ain't cheated since algebra.

MIKE. You're sure gonna look sweet in the ad campaign, sitting on the hood of a brand new Hardbody.

HEATHER. But I'm asleep on my feet! I got this charley-horse, too, working itself up my leg–

MIKE. Whoa, angel! Don't lose the dream! You like riding your bike eight miles every day to the Rib Shack and back?

HEATHER. I got no choice. That Indian giver at the bank, he took back my Honda–

MIKE. All the more reason, baby.

(**HEATHER** *squirms and bites her lip*)

HEATHER. I'm a good girl; I swear.

MIKE. Sometimes "good" don't get the job done.

*(SONG: **BURN THAT BRIDGE**)*

(sings)
TROUBLE SEEMS TO FOLLOW ME
LIKE A LOST AND LONELY DOG
I CAN'T SHAKE IT–NO MATTER HOW I RUN
AND YOU KNOW AND I KNOW
THIS HEAT AIN'T COMING FROM THE SUN
AND THERE'LL BE LIES TO SAY
AND HELL TO PAY
BEFORE THIS DEAL IS DONE

MIKE.
WE'LL BURN THAT BRIDGE WHEN WE GET TO IT
FIND A FIRE WE CAN SET TO IT
TROUBLE'S COMING BUT THE SPARK IS LIT
AND WE'LL BURN THAT BRIDGE WHEN WE GET TO IT
THE SUNLIGHT IN YOUR SMILE
PIERCES ME CLEAN THROUGH
I BEEN ON THIS EARTH AWHILE
I NEVER MET NO ONE LIKE YOU

LORD KNOWS I'M A SINNER
BUT SOMETHING TELLS ME–YOU ARE TOO
AND I'LL PAY TOMORROW FOR WHAT I PRAY
WE'RE ABOUT TO DO

HEATHER. Supposin' we get caught?

MIKE.	**BACKUPS.**
WE'LL BURN THAT BRIDGE WHEN WE GET TO IT.	–BURN THAT BRIDGE WHEN WE GET TO IT.

HEATHER, MIKE.	**BACKUPS.**
FIND A FIRE WE CAN SET TO IT	A FIRE – SET TO IT –
TROUBLE'S COMING, BUT THE	MMMMMMM
SPARK IS LIT	
AND WE'LL BURN THAT BRIDGE	BURN THAT BRIDGE
WHEN WE GET TO IT	

(**MIKE** *pulls a bottle of pills out of his pocket and shakes it.*)

MIKE. Howza 'bout it?

HEATHER. What are those?

MIKE. Energy boosters. Trucker friend of mine, they keep him awake all the way from Birmingham to El Paso.

HEATHER. Can't I just drink coffee?

MIKE. That's amateur, baby.

(sings)
SOMETIMES YOU GOT TO BREAK THE RULES
AND THROW AWAY THE BOOK

HEATHER.
TORCH THE CANDLE AT BOTH ENDS
AND LEAP BEFORE YOU LOOK.

MIKE.
OOOH! YOU MAY BE A LITTLE CRAZY
AND GOD KNOWS I'M NO GREAT CATCH

HEATHER, MIKE.	**BACKUPS.**
BUT YOU PROVIDE THE GASOLINE	YOU PROVIDE THE GASOLINE
AND I'LL PROVIDE THE MATCH!	AND I'LL PROVIDE THE MATCH!

HEATHER, MIKE.
AND WE'LL

HEATHER, MIKE & BACKUPS.
BURN THAT BRIDGE WHEN WE GET TO IT
I KNOW WE SHOULDN'T, BUT THE SPARK IS LIT
IF THIS IS TROUBLE, I DON'T MIND A BIT. AND WE'LL
BURN THAT BRIDGE, BURN THAT BRIDGE
BURN THAT BRIDGE, BURN THAT BRIDGE
BURN THAT BRIDGE, BURN THAT BRIDGE

HEATHER, MIKE.	**BACKUPS.**
BURN THAT BRIDGE	BURN THAT BRIDGE
BURN THAT BRIDGE	BURN THAT BRIDGE
BURN, BURN	BURN, BURN
WE'LL BURN THAT BRIDGE WHEN	BURN THAT BRIDGE
	BURN THAT BRIDGE
WE GET TO IT	BUUUURN, BURN
BURN, BURN	

(**MIKE** *opens the door to the dealership for* **HEATHER.**)

MIKE. Now go out there and win yourself a truck.

MIKE, HEATHER & BACKUPS.
–BURN!

(**HEATHER** *stuffs the meds into her pocket and bounds back to the lot.* **MIKE** *steps out to blow his whistle.*)

MIKE. Time's up! *Hands on!*

(*Time passes; those enchanted hours between late night and early morning.*)

(**GREG** *turns to* **KELLI.**)

GREG. You on vacation or did you have to get off work?

KELLI. My supervisor let me take two sick days. We go a third day, they start docking my pay. You?

GREG. Got laid off from the Stockroom down at Bagley Tractor. Felt like a vacation till they cut off my cable.

KELLI. So what now?

GREG. I put my name in over at Omni Construction, but so far, they ain't called. My Dad says, "These days, you want work, you better fly off to Bangledash or China."

KELLI. You try Kenmar Plastics? They was looking for mold technicians.

GREG. Not no more. Now they're lookin' for bankruptcy lawyers. *(a beat)* You're lucky you got a job.

KELLI. I know. Yeah, I know.

*(SONG: **I'M GONE**)*

(sings)
I WORK AT THE UPS
THE JOB IS PRETTY GOOD I GUESS
I SORT THE PACKAGES, MIDNIGHT TO DAWN.

AROUND HERE YOU CAN BET
THERE'S NO BETTER JOB TO GET
IT'S STEADY WORK YOU CAN RELY UPON.

BUT I CAN ALMOST FEEL THE OCEAN BREEZE
WHEN I READ A LABEL LABELED OVERSEAS
AND SOMETIMES I GET DOWN ON MY KNEES–AND PRAY
JESUS SLIP ME IN THIS PACKAGE
AND SHIP ME FAR AWAY ·
FROM TEETH TO FIX
AND ONE MORE BILL TO PAY.

AND I'M GONE
SO FAR AWAY
GONE
LIKE YESTERDAY
GONE
SO FAST SO FAR
GONE
LIKE A SHOOTING STAR
GONE
LIKE ALL GOOD THINGS

LIKE INNOCENCE
AND SUMMER FLINGS
A DANDELION YOU BLEW A WISH UPON
SCATTERED TO THE FOUR WINDS.

MY MAMA, SHE STILL WORKS TODAY
HER 401K'S BLOWN AWAY
WHEN SHE NEEDS CASH,
SHE FINDS SOMETHING TO PAWN.

SHE'LL PROB'LY NEVER GET THE CHANCE
TO SEE PARIS, TEXAS, OR PARIS, FRANCE
OR A LIFE THAT'S LIVED BEYOND HER OWN FRONT LAWN
AND THAT AIN'T LIVIN'
THAT'S JUST HANGIN' O–ON
I'M GONE!

GREG. So you got it all mapped out, only without a map.

KELLI. *(simply, confidently)* Yep.

GREG.

I ALWAYS HAD THIS DREAM
SINCE I WAS THIRTEEN
TO BE A STUNTMAN ON THE SCREEN

YEAH I BET I'D DO PRETTY GOOD
LEAST I THINK I COULD
IF I COULD GET TO HOLLYWOOD
(spoken) Hey, come with me!

KELLI. What?!

GREG. Dangerous driving all by yourself. I need somebody to keep me awake, change the channel on that Satellite radio–

KELLI. I don't know…

GREG. Don't you want to see palm trees once before you die?

KELLI. Sure, but–

GREG. Gas and grub, fifty-fifty split. You sleep in the cabin, I sleep in the back.

KELLI.	GREG.
I COULD SEE THE PEOPLE THAT I'VE SEEN THERE IN PEOPLE MAGAZINE DANCING WITH CELEBRITIES TIL DAWN! FOR REAL? YOU REALLY THINK I COULD?	TO STUNT IT HELPS TO BE COMPACT I KNOW THAT FOR A FACT AND MAYBE YOU COULD ACT
MIGHT AS WELL WHILE I LOOK GOOD	A GIRL AS BRIGHT AS YOU NO TELLING WHAT YOU'LL DO
WEAR SOME PRETTY CLOTHES AND CARRY ON...	AND DON'T FORGET, I'LL BE THERE TOO

KELLI.
CAUSE I CAN ALMOST FEEL THE OCEAN BREEZE

GREG.
CAN'T YOU FEEL THE OCEAN BREEZE...

KELLI.
WHEN I READ A LABEL LABELLED "OVERSEAS"

GREG.
I'LL JUMP FROM BUILDINGS, SWING FROM TREES...

KELLI.
AND SOMETIMES...

BOTH.
I GET DOWN ON MY KNEES AND PRAY.
IF I WIN THEN I'LL DRIVE YOU
IF YOU WIN, DRIVE ME–OKAY?

SOMEWHERE FAR AWAY FROM HERE
THAT'S WHERE WE'LL FINALLY BE
SOMEBODY THAT NO ONE HERE CAN SEE
I KNOW THERE'S A LIFE OUT THERE FOR ME.

WE'RE GONE!
SO FAR AWAY
GONE
LIKE YESTERDAY
GONE
SO FAST SO FAR
GONE
LIKE A SHOOTING STAR
ONCE IT STREAKS ACROSS A SUMMER SKY
FIREWORKS ON THE 5TH OF JULY
A DANDELION YOU BLEW A WISH UPON

KELLI.
HIT THE PEDAL TO THE METAL

GREG.
BREAK OFF THAT REARVIEW MIRROR

BOTH.
AND EVERYONE WILL KNOW THAT WE WERE HERE
WHEN WE'RE GONE!
WHEN WE'RE GONE!
WHEN WE'RE GONE

(Dawn breaks over the dealership; the sun rises in an orange sky.)

*(**KELLI** props a book against the hood of the truck to read.)*

*(**HEATHER** sets up a tray of make-up, and applies her morning face with one hand.)*

*(**NORMA** listens to her music. RONALD rocks on his heels.)*

*(**GREG**'s head nods forward, then snaps back; he's perilously close to falling asleep.)*

*(**CINDY** enters to relieve **MIKE.**)*

CINDY. Mornin', everybody! Hour number twenty-four!

*(**CINDY** blows her whistle, then crosses into the dealership.)*

You call Tennessee yet? Dan Frankel left three messages for you yesterday–

MIKE. Tell him to relax–

CINDY. I can't keep making up excuses; when you gonna call 'em back?

MIKE. Right now. Let's start their day off right. How many units we move so far?

CINDY. Depends; how'd you do last night?

MIKE. Two "be backs" and a tire kicker had a credit score of two-ninety-five.

CINDY. That it?

MIKE. How'd we do day-time?

CINDY. Paperwork on two hybrids.

MIKE. *(panic rising)* And–?

CINDY. That's it.

MIKE. Bull shit.

CINDY. Not "bull shit," Mike. JACK SHIT.

MIKE. Holy Christ. Fuck me! *Nada?*

CINDY. Look, Mike, this thing ends, and we got a surplus? *They'll say we're nothing but a candy store!* You'll be busting your guts to sell teasers to deadbeats–

MIKE. Damn it, Cindy–

CINDY. –and we'll be a Home Depot faster than you can say "jackrabbit"–

MIKE. *–quit bitchin' like it's all my fault–*

CINDY. I didn't order extra units in a crap economy; you did!

MIKE. –I didn't do it on *purpose–*

CINDY. *(cutting him off)* Tuscan *marble*, Mister? You tell that wife of yours Formica looks just fine.

(She pointedly hands **MIKE** *the bullhorn. He steps outside.)*

MIKE. *Wake up, people! In it to win it!*

(From the truck, **NORMA** *laughs quietly to herself, absorbed in her music. A few of the others notice; her giggles make them smile. A suspect* **JANIS** *rolls her eyes.)*

(**NORMA***'s guffaws slowly grow, gaining momentum, until she erupts in a gale of deep-throated, powerful explosions, doubling over with almost manic glee.*)

JANIS. *(over her shoulder to* **DON***)* There she goes again.

DON. Just ignore it, baby.

GREG. *(to* **JANIS,** *confidentially)* She said when she gets like that, it's the Holy Ghost, takin' possession.

JANIS. What's she gonna do next? Start handlin' snakes or speakin' in tongues?

BENNY. *(to* **J.D.***)* What'd I tell you? Insanity. That's how it starts.

*(SONG: **THE JOY OF THE LORD***)*

NORMA.

HOO!

(laughs)

HEE!

(laughs)

HEY!

(spoken, making a discovery)

Hey.

(singing softly)

WHO WHO WHO?
HAPPY IS HE HE HE!
HAPPY AM I I I!
HAPPY ARE WE WE WE WE

I FEEL THE JOY
I FEEL THE JOY
I FEEL THE JOY IN ME.

(she laughs)

LIFTING MY PAIN
WHEN I NEED IT TO BE
THE JOY OF THE LORD'S IN ME!
WHOO-HOO!

JANIS. What the hell–?

NORMA.

I FEEL NO PAIN!
I FEEL NO PA-IN!
HERE IN HIS GOOD COMPANY!

NORMA. **J.D.**

HEE HEE HOO HOO   SHE FEELS HIS SPIRIT
HEE HOO   IS HERE ON THIS EARTH
HEE HEE HEE HEE

JANIS.

IT SOUNDS TO ME
LIKE SHE'S GIVING BIRTH.

NORMA.

WHOO HOO!

J.D. I'm in.

NORMA.

YAY!!

NORMA & **J.D.**

BLESSED IS HE!
BLESSED IS HE!
GLAD IN THE JOY OF MY LORD'S COMPANY!
WHOOO-OOO

NORMA, J.D. **KELLI.**

OOOOOOOO   SHE'S HAPPY FOR SHUR!
AAAAAHHH **GREG.**

      IF IT WEREN'T FOR ME
      I'D BE BETTING ON HER.

NORMA, J.D., KELLI.

WHOO HOO!

(**NORMA** *and her allies start laughing, giddy from exhaustion and high spirits.*)

NORMA, J.D., JESUS, GREG, **BENNY.**
KELLI.

WHO, WHO, WHO?   YOU GOT TO WONDER
HAPPY IS HE HE HE   WHAT PURPOSE IT SERVES?

      JANIS.

HAPPY AM I I I   I THINK SHE JUST DOES IT
HAPPY ARE WE WE WE!   TO GET ON OUR NERVES.

HAPPY IS   WHAT HAS SHE GOT TO BE
                                          JOYOUS
WHO WHO WHO?   ABOUT?
HAPPY IS HE HE HE   LET HER LAUGH NOW!
HAPPY AM I I I   BUT I'LL LAUGH WHEN
                                          SHE'S
HAPPY ARE WE WE WE!   OUT!

NORMA.

DO YOU FEEL HIS HOLY JOY?

ALL. *(except* **CHRIS** *and* **JANIS***)*

YES!

NORMA.

DO YOU FEEL HIS HOLY JOY?

ALL. *(except* **CHRIS** *and* **JANIS***)*

YE-EE-EE-ES!

NORMA & HEATHER.

DO YOU FEEL THE POWER
OF HIS HOLINESS?
DO YOU FEEL HIS HOLY JOY?

ALL. *(except* **CHRIS***)*

YES!

NORMA.	**ALL BUT CHRIS.**
I GET A POWERFUL FEELING	
	I FEEL THE JOY!
I FEEL IT E-VE-RY DAY!	
	I FEEL THE JOY!
HE'S GONNA LIFT MY SOUL	
	I FEEL THE JOY!
AND TAKE MY PAIN AWAY	
	I FEEL THE JOY!
HE COMES TO ME	
	I FEEL THE JOY!
WHEN I NEED HIM THE MOST	
	I FEEL THE JOY!
I FEEL THE HEAVENLY JOY	

	I FEEL THE JOY!
FROM MY HEAVENLY GHOST!	
	I FEEL THE JOY!
I AIN'T TIRED NO MORE	
	I FEEL THE JOY!
I AIN'T NO WAY SORE!	
	I FEEL THE JOY!
THE DEVIL WILL NEVER DEVIL	
	I FEEL THE JOY!
NORMA NO MORE!	
	NORMA NO MORE!
NORMA NO MORE!	
	NORMA NO MORE!
NORMA NO MORE!	
	NORMA NO MORE!
THE DEVIL WILL NEVER DEVIL	
NORMA NO MORE!	NORMA NO MORE!

(Exuberantly, they begin to "play" the truck, getting percussive tonalities on the hub cabs, grill, hood, windshield wipers, and from the occasional horn blasts.)

ALL *but* **CHRIS**.

I FEEL THE JOY!
I FEEL THE JOY!
I FEEL THE JOY!
I FEEL THE JOY!
I FEEL THE JOY!
I FEEL THE JOY!

NORMA.

THE JOY OF THE LORD!

(The song ends in celebration; suddenly the whole band kicks back in.)

*(In the midst of all the jubilation, **CHRIS** paces back and forth like a panther until he can't contain his rage any longer.)*

CHRIS. *Ahhhh! Shut the fuck up!*

(stunned silence)

JANIS. Listen, Mister. You've got no right to talk to her like that.

CHRIS. She's got no right shoving her goddamn Bible in my face.

J.D. Son, you leave that language in the barracks where it belongs–

CHRIS. Screw you, old man.

BENNY. *(truly angry)* Yo. Private. You think just cuz you ate some sand over there, you're some kinda tough guy? Some kinda hero? My son–

CHRIS. Oh, your son? You wanna talk about your son? *I know about your son, asshole–?*

BENNY. *You don't know shit, punk–*

(NORMA can't bear it any longer.)

NORMA. Leave him be. Just leave him be.

(A pall falls over the CONTESTANTS. They avoid making eye contact with CHRIS. But NORMA stares at him with compassion.)

NORMA. *(cont.)* How long have you been home?

(CHRIS swallows, embarrassed.)

My nephew Hector came back six months ago. Army, first cavalry. Trained down at Fort Hood. Before his deployment, he used to go to church, every Sunday. Now he's home, he's got no use for the Bible, either. *(a beat)* God forgives us, but forgiving Him can take a very long time.

(CHRIS tries to piece together an answer but words fail him.)

CHRIS. Mam, I…ah. See, I–

NORMA. Shhh. It's all right.

CHRIS. No. No, it's not.

*(SONG: **STRONGER**)*

CHRIS. *(cont.) (sings)*

I WAS CUTTING UP AND ACTING LIKE A FOOL
THE DAY THOSE TWO RECRUITERS SHOWED UP AT OUR
  SCHOOL.
AND I SWORE HE WAS LOOKING RIGHT AT ME
WHEN HE TOLD ME I COULD BE ALL I COULD BE.

I WAS A BABY, NEWLY MARRIED
WITH THE BABY THAT SHE CARRIED
AND I WAS LOST AND LOOKING FOR MY WAY
AND HE ASKED ME IF I LOVED THE USA.

AND GOD I HOPED THEY'D TAKE ME
CAUSE HE SWORE THEY'D MAKE ME

STRONGER
THAN THAT COWARD I KEPT HID
STRONGER
TURN THAT 98 POUND KID
INTO A STRONG MAN
AND BY GOD THEY DID

(With his free hand, he slides off his sunglasses and hangs them off his t-shirt collar.)

I WISHED I'D HELD MY WIFE A LITTLE LONGER
BUT IT ONLY MADE ME STRONGER
IT ONLY MADE ME STRONGER.

NOW I'VE MARCHED TIL I WAS BLIND THROUGH DESERT
  SANDS
SLEPT IN MUD WITH SOMEONE'S BLOOD UPON MY HANDS
SWEPT THROUGH MINE FIELDS,
STAYED UP FIGHTING FOUR NIGHTS STRAIGHT.
HELPED A WOMAN, SEEN HER LOOK AT ME WITH HATE.

ONCE I SAW A YOUNG GIRL DYING
FATHER HOLDING HER AND CRYING
HE BEGGED ME PLEASE TO HELP, WHAT COULD I DO?
SHE WAS DEAD AND IF I'D STAYED, I'D BE DEAD TOO.
I'VE SEEN THINGS PAST ALL KNOWING
YET I KEPT ON GROWING

STRONGER
THAN I WAS THE DAY BEFORE
STRONGER
LIKE YOU HAVE TO BE IN WAR
I KNOW
WHAT THE FUTURE HOLDS IN STORE
AND I DON'T FEAR IT ANY LONGER
HELL, IT ONLY MAKES ME STRONGER

STANDING HERE BESIDE THIS TRUCK
I KNOW JUST HOW TO BE!
ALL MY TRAINING'S COMING BACK
SO QUICK AND EASILY
I NEVER FELT MORE SURE
I NEVER FELT MORE FREE!
...IT'S JUST EV'RY OTHER PART OF LIFE
THAT'S BAFFLING TO ME.

CHRIS.	CONTESTANTS, DON.
STRONGER	OOOOOOHHHH
I JUST TELL MYSELF I CAN	
BE STRONGER	OOOOOOHHHH
PROVIDER, HUSBAND,	
FATHER, MAN	
BUT SOMEWHERE	SOMEWHERE OOOOOOOO
I LOST TRACK OF THE PLAN	
I DON'T REALLY HAVE ONE	
DAY LONGER	
ALL I NEED TO BE IS	

CONTESTANTS, DON.
STRONGER, STRONGER, STRONGER

CHRIS.
...HOLD DOWN A 9 TO 5

CONTESTANTS, DON.
STRONGER, STRONGER

CHRIS.
...MORE THAN HALF ALIVE

CHRIS.	CONTESTANTS, DON.
HOW COME	HOW COME

I'M THE ONE GOT TO   AHHHHH
    SURVIVE,
WHEN I DON'T FEEL LIKE
    LIVING ANY LONGER?

ALL.

I DON'T FEEL LIKE LIVING ANY LONGER.
I DON'T FEEL LIKE LIVING ANY LONGER!

CHRIS.   **CONTESTANTS, DON.**

HOW COME   OOOOOOOO
I'M THE ONE GOT TO   OOOOOOOO
    SURVIVE   OOOOOOOO
WHEN I DON'T FEEL LIKE
    LIVING ANY LONGER?

CHRIS.

IF YOU'RE NOT GOING TO TAKE ME
THEN OH GOD WON'T YOU MAKE ME
STRONGER?

(The other **CONTESTANTS** *stare at him, moved;* **NORMA**
is especially touched.)

*(***CHRIS** *becomes self-conscious; he's told too much. He
slides his shades back on in an effort to reclaim his
dignity. He opens his mouth to say something, censors
himself, and bolts off.)*

*(***FRANK** *presses his jingle button.)*

JINGLE.

FLOYD KING NISSAN
PICK UP AND GO!

FRANK. Mr. Chris Alvaro, down for the count–

*(***BENNY** *gives a high-pitched laugh.)*

BENNY. –I sure didn't see that comin'–

NORMA. You show him respect.

BENNY. For what? Dropping off?

J.D. *(sotto voce, to his friend)* Come on, Benny. Kid went off
to war.

BENNY. *(undaunted)* Big whup, so did mine.

J.D. Then show him the respect you'd show your own—

BENNY. Mine didn't come home mealy-mouthed, crying about it. I never ONCE heard my son complain.

(The **CONTESTANTS** *pipe up in an angry cacophony.*)

KELLI. You oughta be disqualified anyway—

JANIS. —you ask me, he's a no-good weasel—

HEATHER. —you had your turn, you already won—

JESUS. *Pa' que quieres dos trockas?*

DON. Now that's what I call poor sportsmanship—

GREG. Kinda early in the game to call somebody else out—

BENNY. You people done?

(SONG: ***IF YOU CAN'T HUNT WITH THE BIG DOGS***)

(*sings*)

WE'VE HAD OUR LITTLE MEET N' GREET
WE'VE HAD OUR LITTLE FUN
BUT IT'S LIKE THE MOVIE 'HIGHLANDER'
"THERE CAN BE ONLY ONE."

(*calling after* **CHRIS**)

YOU GOT TO HAVE THE HEART FOR BATTLE, SON
LIKE OUR FOREFATHERS DID
YOU CAN'T BE NO WET-BEHIND-THE-EARS
SNOT-NOSED LITTLE KID

(*back to the others*)

WELL DOES THAT SOUND TOO ROUGH? WELL TOO BAD TOUGH
YOU BETTER GET READY FOR MORE!
THAT WAS TAME, JUST THE NAME OF THE GAME
WHAT THE HELL YOU THINK WE CAME HERE FOR?

IF YOU CAN'T HUNT WITH THE BIG DOGS
BETTER GET OUT THE WAY *HA!*
I AIN'T COME HERE TO MAKE NO FRIENDS
I DIDN'T COME HERE TO PLAY
YOU CAN'T GET THE THRILL OF THE CHASE AND KILL

WHEN YOU'RE CRYING THERE IN YOUR CUPS
IF YOU CAN'T HUNT WITH THE BIG DOGS
STAY ON THE PORCH WITH THE PUPS.

KELLI.

I'M GETTING TIRED OF YOU AND YOUR MOUTH
YOUR GUMS KEEP FLAPPING
DON'T YOU EVER STOP TALKING?!

BENNY.

IT'S LIKE THE FIRST TIME THAT YOU KILL A DEER
AND IT LOOKS YOU IN THE EYE
THAT INTENSE EXHILARATION
AS YOU WATCH THAT CREATURE DIE!
YOU WATCH THAT CREATURE DIE!

GREG. *(to* **BENNY***)*

YOU DON'T SCARE ME MISTER
I'LL BE HERE ALL NIGHT
I AIN'T AFRAID TO KICK YOUR ASS
YOU WANT TO FIGHT? LET'S FIGHT!

JANIS. *(to* **BENNY***)*

WELL YOU TALK REAL BIG
LIKE YOU OWN THIS RIG
THE MASTER WITH THE MASTER PLAN
BUT I SAW YOUR WIFE IN THAT TRUCK YOU WON
AND SHE WAS DRIVING WITH ANOTHER MAN!

BENNY. *(spoken)* Even when you all drop off–*when each and every one of you is ancient history*–I'll stay on. By myself. Until I beat the world's record!

(sings)

AND IF YOU'RE GONNA SQUIRM
WHEN YOU EAT THE WORM
YOU BETTER STICK TO YOUR 7 UPS!
IF YOU CAN'T HUNT WITH THE BIG DOGS

BENNY.	**CONTESTANTS, DON.**
...STAY ON THE PORCH	OOOOOOOOOOHHH
WITH THE PUPPIES	
WADE IN THE POND WITH	
THE GUPPIES	

RUN TO YOUR MA WITH THE WUSSIES	OOOHH
GET IN THE BARN WITH THE PUSSIES!	WOAH!
…STAY ON THE PORCH WITH THE PUPS!	

DON.

HE GOT A FILTHY MOUTH!
AND A FILTHY MIND!
THE MAN AIN'T NOTHIN' BUT A MULE'S BEHIND!

BENNY.

STAY ON THE PORCH WITH THE PUPPIES!

JANIS.

YEAH I SAW YOUR WIFE IN THAT TRUCK OF YOURS
AND SHE WAS DRIVING WITH ANOTHER MAN!

BENNY.

STAY ON THE PORCH WITH THE PUPS!

GREG, HEATHER

OLD MAN! OLD OLD MAN!
YOU'RE GONNA DIE SOON!
YOU'RE AN OLD, OLD MAN!

BENNY.

STAY ON THE PORCH WITH THE PUPPIES!

KELLI.	**JANIS.**	**HEATHER, GREG.**
I'M SO TIRED OF YOU AND YOUR MOUTH!	YEAH I SAW…	OLD MAN…

BENNY.	**JESUS.**
STAY ON THE PORCH WITH THE PUPS	I'M GONNA KICK YOUR ASS NOW

J.D.	NORMA.	JANIS.	KELLI.	HEATHER, GREG.
CUERVO!	OH LORD FORGIVE HIM	YEAH I SAW...	I'M SO TIRED...	OLD MAN OLD OLD MAN

BENNY.   JESUS.

STAY ON THE PORCH WITH   I'LL SHOW YOU WHO'S A
    THE PUPPIES   TOUGH MAN!

(the following lyrics are sung simultaneously)

J.D.	NORMA.	JANIS.
CUERVO!	OH LORD FORGIVE HIM	YEAH I SAW...

KELLI.	HEATHER, GREG.	JESUS.
I'M SO TIRED...	OLD MAN YOU'RE GONNA DIE SOON!	I'LL SHOW YOU...

*(In the dealership, **MIKE** and **CINDY** notice the bedlam outside. **CINDY** passes the megaphone to **MIKE**. He barrels onto the lot.)*

BENNY.

YOU BETTER STAY ON THE PORCH WITH THE PUPS!

*(**MIKE** raises his megaphone to shout above the tumult)*

MIKE. *FIFTEEN! YOU HEAR ME, PEOPLE? WE'RE ON A FIFTEEN!*

(sudden blackout)

END OF ACT ONE

ACT TWO

(The sunlight is blinding; it bounces off the waxy car finishes on the lot so brightly it hurts.)

*(The **CONTESTANTS** have disappeared to use the outdoor restrooms and re-group during the break.)*

*(**FRANK**, however, is ready to rock. He has a guitar slung over his shoulder and he's wearing his best shit-kicker boots. Together with **MIKE**, he plans to get the audience stoked. They're two mid-life white guys who still play air guitar in their wood-paneled rec rooms, and this is their moment to shine.)*

FRANK. Ah-one, two, Ah-one–

*(And the **BAND** kicks in.)*

MIKE. WHOO-WHEE! It's HOT. *(to a woman in the crowd)* Kinda hot where your thighs stick together like rubber. Don't they, mam?

(to a man) And that hair gel you put in this morning to look slick for the ladies…it's slidin' down your neck, am I right?

(to everyone) So why don't ya'll go cool off in the show room? Prices as low as the temperature's high! Speaking of scorchers, we got a treat for you now. A song, written especially for the contest by our very own Mr. Frank Nugent–!

FRANK. How ya'll doing'? Download this baby offa dubya dubya dubya Floyd King dot com! Seventh inning stretch people, shake 'em if you got 'em!

*(SONG: **HANDS ON A HARDBODY**)*

77

FRANK. *(cont.) (sings)*
> WELL, SHE'S A BOOT SCOOTIN'
> ROOTIN TOOTIN
> LOW RIDIN'
> HIGH FALUTIN
> PRETTY LITTLE SO AND SO
>
> SHE'S A DROP DEAD
> CHERRY RED
> EXTRA ROOM THERE IN HER BED
> WRAPPED UP IN A CHRISTMAS BOW
>
> ONE LOOK AND YOU'RE A GONER
> CAUSE SHE'S GOT NO MILES ON HER
> AND YOU CAN DRIVE HER HOME FOR FREE
>
> FROM THE SHOWROOM TO THE STANDS
> EVEN FANS
> GOT THEIR PLANS
> EVERYBODY WANTS THEIR HANDS ON A
> HARDBODY!

BOTH.
> EVERYBODY'S SCREAMIN' FOR THE HARDBODY
> DREAMIN THAT THEY'RE DRIVIN HOME THAT HOT ROD
>   HOTTIE
> LITTLE BIT A DREAMIN' NEVER HURT NOBODY
> MAN SHE'S COMIN' HOME WITH ME!

MIKE. Let's welcome back our contestants!

> *(Lead by an intrepid* **CINDY,** *the* **CONTESTANTS** *shuffle out in the saddest line dance ever. They've all spent two days on their feet in debilitating conditions. Still, they try to dance.)*

> *(***JESUS** *limps forward on his boots, his feet tender with blisters.)*

> *(***JANIS** *clings to her husband* **DON** *for support, like a life-sized puppet he has to manipulate.)*

> *(***GREG***'s had so much Red Bull that he's doused with sweat and he's twitching.)*

(**KELLI** *keeps nodding off, then jolting awake as she walks.*)

(**NORMA** *has her earphones in place, dancing to her own rhythm.*)

(**J.D.** *has a cold towel around his neck, and a cigarette dripping out of his mouth. As he walks, he sways his hips to song's rhythm.*)

(*Still in fighting mode,* **BENNY** *has a bandana around his head, and rolled up his pants legs, his arms raised in a victory dance.*)

(**HEATHER,** *high on uppers, kicks her legs with abandon in a frenzy of artificially-induced energy.*)

BOTH.

AND YOU KNOW UNDER THE HOOD
SHE'LL BE LOOKIN JUST AS GOOD
BUT MAN SHE'S JUST TOO HOT TO TOUCH

FRANK.

IT'S A CHANCE A TEXAN TAKES
SHE MIGHT MAKE YOU PUMP THE BRAKES
BUT–

BOTH.

–SHE ALWAYS COMES THROUGH IN THE CLUTCH!

MIKE.

SHE'LL KEEP YOU STANDING HERE FOR HOURS
WITHOUT BENEFIT OF SHOWERS
JUST TO PLAY A GAME OF WAIT AND SEE
IT LOOKS EASY BUT IT AIN'T

FRANK.

TAKES THE PATIENCE OF A SAINT

BOTH.

IT'S LIKE WATCHIN DRYIN PAINT
TO WIN THAT HARDBODY!
EVERYBODY'S GUNNIN FOR THE HARDBODY
FRYIN' IN THE SUN HERE FOR THAT HOT ROD HOTTIE
YOU CAN KEEP YOUR PORSCHES AND YOUR MASERATI

FRANK.
> MAN, SHE'S COMIN' HOME WITH ME!

MIKE.
> SHE'S COMIN' HOME WITH ME!

BOTH.
> SHE'S COMIN' HOME WITH ME!
> SHE'S A BOOT SCOOTIN ROOTIN TOOTIN
> HIGH FALUTIN' HOTTIE
> NOW WHO'S GONNA GET THEIR HANDS ON THAT
>   HARDBODY?

MIKE. Come on, tell me who's gonna win it? I can't hear you!

> *(The* **CONTESTANTS** *respond with lackluster, half-hearted ad libs.)*

CONTESTANTS. Me! I will! Me! No, Me!

MIKE. *(blowing his whistle)* Hands on!

> *(***EVERYONE*** resumes their place at the truck.* **MIKE** *goes inside.)*

J.D. *(on the verge of sleep, to* **BENNY***)* Cuervo.

> *(***BENNY*** slaps* **J.D.** *awake.)*

> *(***CINDY*** enters the lot from the dealership, clipboard in hand, and makes a bee-line for* **JESUS***.)*

CINDY. JESUS. darlin'.

JESUS. *Si?*

CINDY. Sweetie, if you win this thing, you know I'm gonna have to see somethin'.

JESUS. *Como?*

CINDY. Honey, I think you know.

JESUS. No.

CINDY. *Identificación.* A green card, maybe?

> *(SONG: **BORN IN LAREDO**)*

> *(Caught off-guard by* **CINDY***'s request, thoughts race through* **JESUS***' head.)*

JESUS. *(sings)*
> YOU LOOK AT ME
> AND I SEE WHAT YOU SEE

CINDY. *Carta verde?*

JESUS.
> SOMEONE WHO COMES TO YOUR COUNTRY
> AND TAKES ALL YOUR JOBS
> WHO'S LIVING HERE ILLEGALLY

CINDY. *Comprende?*

JESUS.
> DID I FLOAT ON A RAFT
> CROSS THE RIO GRANDE?
> OR HIDE UNDER CARDBOARD AND HAY
> IN AN OLD FLAT-BED TRUCK
> TO STEAL INTO YOUR LAND?

> *(**JESUS** nods toward **BENNY**)*

He wins, you gonna ask him?

CINDY. To see his driver's license, yes.

JESUS.
> YOU LOOK AT ME
> AND YOU THINK I RUN DOPE
> A KILLER, MY GANG'S NAME CARVED INTO MY ARM
> JUST A MONSTER, UNWORTHY OF HOPE.
> OR YOU LOOK AT ME
> AND THINK, HE'S NOT TOO BRIGHT
> LET HIM CUT GRASS, BUS DISHES
> SHINE SHOES AT THE MALL,
> CLEAN THE STALLS AT THE GREYHOUND AT NIGHT.
> YOU WISH THAT I'D NEVER COME
> FROM THE COUNTRY I'M FROM

> BUT I'M BORN IN LAREDO
> MY SISTER WAS BORN IN FORT WORTH
> BORN IN LAREDO
> AMERICAN BY BIRTH

JESUS.	BACKUPS.
I WENT TO SCHOOL	
AND I DREAMED OF A	
HOME AND A CAR	
AND I'M BORN IN LAREDO	
EVERY INCH THE TEXAN	AAAAA-AAAAAA-
YOU ARE	AAAHHHHHH
I LOOK AT YOU	
AND I SEE A BRICK WALL	
SOMEONE WHO'S MADE UP	OOO
HIS MIND	
BASED ON JUST WHAT HE	OOO
SEES	
AND I SEE SHE SEES	AAAAAAHHH
NOTHING AT ALL	
CAUSE I LOOK AT YOU	
DO YOU KNOW WHAT I SEE?	
SOMEONE WHO COMES	OOO
FROM A FAMILY	
THAT SAILED LONG AGO	OOO
IN SEARCH OF A NEW LIFE,	AAAAAHH
LIKE ME	
DID THEY COME HERE	
ALONE?	
WERE THEY VIEWED WITH	
ALARM?	
DID THEY WORK TO THE	
BONE FOR THEIR	
FAMILY	
DREAMING OF LAND AND A	
SMALL WORKING FARM?	
IF THEY CAME HERE TODAY	AAH
I WOULD PRAY FOR THEIR	OOO
SOUL	
AND HOPE THEY RUN FAST	
OR THEY'D NEVER GET	
PAST	

THE VOLUNTEER BORDER   AAAAA-AAAAA-AAAAA-
    PATROL.   AAAHH
MY PARENTS THEY SLEPT
    ON THE FLOOR
AND THEY HOPED I'D HAVE
    MORE

MEN.

HOPED I'D HAVE MORE

WOMEN.

HOPED I'D HAVE MORE

JESUS.   **BACKUPS.**

AND I'M BORN IN LAREDO   BORN
WHERE I LEARNED HOW TO   OOOOOOOOO
    FIGHT MY OWN FIGHTS
RAISED IN LAREDO   RAISED
BEER AND HOT DOGS AND
    FRIDAY NIGHT LIGHTS
MY GRANDFATHER CAME   AAAAAAAAAAHHHHH
MADE A RAFT FROM THE
    HOOD OF A CAR   AAAAAAAAAAHHHHH
BUT I'M BORN IN LAREDO   BORN IN LAREDO–
                         OOOOOOOHHH

EVERY INCH THE TEXAN
    YOU ARE

                        AAAAAAAAA-HHH
                        AAAAAAAAA-HHH
                        WHOAAAAA

(the song concludes.)

(Time passes; morning of the third day dawns.)

HEATHER. Mornin' number three, ya'll!

(She bends over in front of the rear-view mirror so she can freshen her make-up.)

JANIS. *(to JESUS)* Last break, you know what she was up to? Sittin' in a brand new Z-coupe, engine on, with her curlin' iron plugged into the dash, doin' her hair. *(genuinely baffled)* Who for? We know what she looks like.

J.D. Ginny, get me another ice pack, will ya–Ginny? Hello? *(realizing she's not there)* Oh. Right. Shame on me.

(sings)

WHEN I WAS TWENTY-THREE AND SHE WAS SEVENTEEN
SHE WAS A MOVIE STAR OUT OF A MAGAZINE
AND I WAS JIMMY DEAN AND STEVE MCQUEEN
ROLLED INTO ONE

WELL SHE LOOKS THE SAME, AT LEAST TO ME
BUT I'M NOT THE MAN I USED TO BE

SHE MUST HAVE BEEN SO FRIGHTENED
AS I LAY THERE IN THAT BED
I WISH THAT I COULD TAKE BACK
EVERY AWFUL THING I SAID

*(**BENNY** snaps **J.D.** out of it.)*

BENNY. Whoa. Kimosabe. Check out the bleachers. They're comin' out the woodwork now. Just to watch us suffer. To pray that we fall. It's gladiator time, people.

*(Suddenly, **JANIS** blurts out.)*

JANIS. Ms. Barnes! Ms. Barnes!

*(**HEATHER** cries out defensively.)*

HEATHER. What on earth did I do this time?

*(In the dealership, **CINDY** grimaces at **MIKE**, bracing herself.)*

CINDY. Christ, just what we need. It's that Curtis woman again.

MIKE. Who's she doggin' now? Heather?

CINDY. I'll deal with it–

MIKE. *(sharply) No!* Let me.

*(**CINDY** gives **MIKE** a curious look; he goes out to answer **JANIS**' cry.)*

Yes, Janis?

JANIS. She done it, second time today. Had her lipstick in her right hand, and lifted up her left hand to take the top off so she could screw it outta the tube–

HEATHER. I did not!

JANIS. Was too–I saw it–

HEATHER. That's not true–

JANIS. *(emphatic) I saw! You was screwing it outta the tube–*

MIKE. All right, people, calm down. Now I been watching on the monitor inside–

JANIS. –both hands was off the truck, ten seconds or more–

MIKE. –I didn't see anything like that–

JANIS. –I'm two feet away, how far are you?–

MIKE. –if you'd worry 'bout yourself as much as you worry 'bout others–

JANIS. Just look at her lips! Red as roses. You think she did that single-handed?

MIKE. Ms. Stovall, did you take your hand off the truck?

HEATHER. *(also rote)* No, sir.

MIKE. *(to* **JANIS***)* One more false alarm, and I'm gonna have to disqualify you.

(**HEATHER** *narrows her eyes at* **JANIS***, fuming.* **JANIS** *is red with rage.)*

JANIS. It's a fix! Whole thing's a goddamn fix!

(**DON** *rushes on from the side-lines.)*

DON. What happened, angel?

(SONG: ***IT'S A FIX****)*

JANIS.

THAT YOUNG LADY THERE
WITH THE LEGS AND THE HAIR
WELL, SHE'S CHEATED ON THIS SINCE DAY ONE!
THEM DAMN CROOKED JUDGES
ALLOW ALL HER FUDGES
PRETENDING THEY AIN'T SEEN 'EM DONE!

FAIR IS FAIR
AND THIS AIN'T FAIR
I'LL TEAR HER HAIR OUT
I DON'T CARE

I'M WEARY
AND MY NECK'S GOT CRICKS
PLUMB WORE OUT FROM THESE POLITICS!
NOW ME AND DON ARE REDNECKS
BUT WE AIN'T NO GODDAMN HICKS–IT'S A FIX!
IT'S ALL A FIX!
(spoken) I've seen it everywhere! Everywhere!
(sings)

I WENT DOWN TO SNAP
TRIED TO GET ME SOME FOOD STAMPS
DOWN TO MY VERY LAST QUARTER
THEY GAVE ME SOME CRAP
WE WAS LIVING TOO WELL
WE WAS LIVING ON

JANIS & DON.

POPCORN AND WATER

JANIS.

AND THOSE PEOPLE IN HEALTH CARE?
HELL–THEY'RE 0 FOR 2 THERE.
YOU'RE SICK? WE DON'T CARE–

JANIS & DON.

ROT IN BED!

JANIS.

THEY TURNED MAMA DOWN
'PRE-EXISTING CONDITIONS'
YEAH–SHE WAS OLD
NOW SHE'S DEAD!

JANIS & DON.

EVERYWHERE YOU GO, IT'S ALL THE SAME
WE'RE JUST PAWNS IN THIS CROOKED GAME
THE LITTLE ONES GET CHEATED
AND WHO'S TO BLAME?
JUST DIRTY LITTLE MINDS
PLAYING DIRTY LITTLE TRICKS
OH…IT'S A FIX! IT'S A FIX!

(**JANIS** *hops up onto the rear fender to make her case to
the crowd.*)

JANIS.

ALL Y'ALL KNOW I AIN'T NO LIAR
ANYWHERE THERE'S SMOKE, THERE'S FIRE
Y'ALL DONE SLIPPED UP THAT'S COMPETED
AND I SHOULD KNOW BECAUSE I CHEATED.
I'M JUST ONE MORE FOOL THAT'S CHEATED!
(spoken) My sunglasses was slippin' off my nose, and I took my hand off by mistake!

(sings)

THAT'S RIGHT, I MESSED UP
LEAST I HAVE FESSED UP
THOUGH NOBODY SAW MY HANDS ROAM
I COULD HAVE WON IT
BUT GOD SEEN I DONE IT
SO GOD DUMMIT, I'M GOING HOME!

FRANK. Going home?

JANIS.

I'M GOING HOME!

*(With that **JANIS** raises her hand off the truck, tears off the glove and throws it contemptuously on the ground.)*

FRANK. *(to **DON**)* Sad to see your wife give up?

DON. *(proudly)* She ain't *giving* up; she's *standing* up.

JANIS.

I'LL LEAVE WITH NOTHING!
BUT I GOT MY PRIDE
LEAST I WAS HONEST AND I TOLD I LIED
THE WHOLE WORLD'S CROOKED
AND THEN ONCE YOU'VE DIED

YOU EVEN GOT TO BRIBE THE BOATMAN
AT THE RIVER STYX!
OH...IT'S A FIX!

DON.

IT'S A FIX!

JANIS & DON.

IT'S A FIX!

(Like one of the mythical Furies, **JANIS** *exits with* **DON** *on her heels)*

*(***FRANK*** cues the jingle.)*

JINGLE.
FLOYD KING NISSAN
PICK UP AND GO!

FRANK. Ms. Janis Curtis, bidding the contest a fond farewell.

*(***MIKE*** turns to leave, but* **KELLI** *leaps to* **JANIS**' *defense.)*

KELLI. I've seen people take their hands off. So's Greg.

GREG. People in the pit seen it too, just ask 'em–

KELLI. You can lift your hand so nobody sees then put it right back, it's not so hard to do–

MIKE. Look, people. There's an awful lot of "he did, she said, we did, this did–"

KELLI. What are we supposed to do? Police ourselves?

GREG. *(sarcastic)* I didn't know it was an "honor system–"

*(***MIKE*** turns to* **CINDY.***)*

MIKE. Ms. Barnes?

CINDY. *(a low hiss)* What?

MIKE. *(hissing back) You're "Rules and Regulations."*

CINDY. Okay. Listen up. Mike and I, we're just doing this as a service to the dealership. And to you all. I'll admit, we are not professionals. We did not go to the...the... *(flustered)* ..."The Judging School of Hardbody Hands of America." But this contest couldn't happen without us.

NORMA. Janis was honest. She may not win this truck because of it, but she was.

CINDY. The thing you gotta understand? Me and Mike, hard as we try, we only got one pair of eyes. And there's how many of you all left? I've lost count. Seven? *(clearing her throat)* So what we're gonna do now is *tighten the rules.*

MIKE. They been tight already–

CINDY. That's right, they have! But starting right now, it's crackdown time.

(*Again,* **CINDY** *singles out* **JESUS.**)

Jesus, honey. Look at me. *Comprende?*

(**JESUS**'*jaw clenches.*)

JESUS. *Señora, tu tienes un perro?*

CINDY. Excuse me?

JESUS. Do you have a dog?

(**CINDY** *stares at him, confused.*)

(*forceful but without rancor*) Because if I win this game, I get my diploma. Maybe one day in the future, your dog, he gets sick. You drive a long way, through neighborhoods you don't know. The Animal Clinic. Open all night. I'm there, in my white coat. You're surprised. You give your dog to me, and what do I do? (*a beat*) I take his life in my hands. *Comprende?*

CINDY. (*a strained smile*) My goodness. Who's to say? (*trying to rally them*) Okay! Who's gonna end up winning this truck?

(*a few meagre cries*)

VARIOUS CONTESTANTS. Me. No, me. Me.

CINDY. (*joyless*) Then get to it!

(**MIKE** *and* **CINDY** *retreat back to the dealership. Once they're gone,* **EVERYONE** *stares down* **HEATHER.**)

HEATHER. (*meekly*) What're you all looking at me for?

(*meanwhile inside*)

CINDY. What is going on out there, Mike?

MIKE. (*evasively*) They are one tough crowd. *Man.* Like wranglin' alligators–

CINDY. Folks think this contest is crooked, we're screwed–

MIKE. –maybe we're screwed already–

CINDY. How they gonna trust us to draw up a sales contract or a warranty–

MIKE. *(bitterly)* Lucky for us, we haven't had to–

CINDY. But when we do–

MIKE. "If" we do is more like it–

> (**CINDY** *slams her clipboard to the floor.*)

CINDY. Dammit, Mike! I got the twins sleeping on a sofa bed! Eatin' oatmeal for dinner! Carl is *eight months* behind in his child support, and my next paycheck's already spent, twice over–!

> (**CINDY** *is choking back tears, furious now.*)

You throw this thing, I will throw you–

MIKE. *(flaring defensively)* Who's got seniority here, you or me?

CINDY. I talked to Tennessee, you didn't.

> (*This catches* **MIKE.**)

MIKE. And–?

CINDY. Our travel rate off the lot this month? It's the lowest in East Texas–

MIKE. *The lowest?*

CINDY. They're movin' twice as many units in Tyler. Dan had a few choice words for you. He said you'd "dishonored" Nissan.

MIKE. "Dishonored?"

CINDY. He chose that word special. He said that's how executives talk overseas. It means you have screwed the pooch in Japanese.

> (**MIKE** *is shaken.* **CINDY** *gives him a withering look.*)

In Toyko, men throw themselves on swords for less.

MIKE. *(angling to leave)* My shift's way past over–

CINDY. Oh no, you don't. It's you 'n me. Together. Till the bitter end, you hear me?

> (*Time passes into mid-day. At the DJ's booth,* **FRANK** *conducts another interview.*)

FRANK. Here with me now, Dr. Charles Stokes from Le Tourneau University.

DR. STOKES. Pleasure to be here.

FRANK. So. Doc. Any health hazards in a contest like this?

DR. STOKES. Sleep deprivation, for a start.

FRANK. Folks Google that, what'll they find?

DR. STOKES. It's a common torture technique used by the Chinese to persecute the Falun Gong, and by our very own CIA to break Al Qaeda operatives.

FRANK. No shit.

DR. STOKES. Brain function deteriorates. The body experiences tremors, hallucinations, even psychosis.

FRANK. *(worried)* Nobody's ever, say, died. Have they?

DR. STOKES. Lab rats die after thirty-two days. But a human being? *(darkly)* I wouldn't press it.

(Time passes, and we're in the wee hours of fourth day.)

(HEATHER *whispers to* **JESUS.)**

HEATHER. Look! I swear that's him.

JESUS. Who?

HEATHER. Soldier boy. Over there, walking up and down, past the Hatchbacks like a ghost. When was it he fell off?

(KELLI *tilts forward, her eyes flickering closed. Suddenly her knees buckle. With his free hand,* **GREG** *props her up.* **KELLI** *shoots him a grateful look, then shakes her head furiously to stay alert.)*

GREG. Not now. You made it more than half-way.

J.D. How long?

BENNY. Going on seventy-one hours.

J.D. Sun goes up and comes down, but that K-Mart sign across the way? It stays lit.

BENNY. Feels like I spent my whole damn life right here, on this sorry patch o' concrete.

J.D. *(to* **BENNY***)* Funny, ain't it? American dream, a Japanese car?

(BENNY *answers with a rueful smile.)*

You from Longview?

BENNY. Kilgore, fifteen miles southwest. You?

J.D. North Center Street. Other night, I went to see the house where I was born. Got lost. Wound up on a dead-end road, back of a recycling plant. *(a beat)* Scared the crap out of me.

*(SONG: **USED TO BE**)*

(sings)

THAT SIGN UP THERE SAYS "NISSAN"
BUT WHERE IT'S WORN AWAY
YOU CAN STILL READ "CHEVROLET"
BOUGHT MY 86 CAMARO HERE
I STILL MISS THAT CAR TODAY.

AND OVER THERE WHERE THE STOP-AND-GO SITS
WAS THE MOM & POP WITH THE SLOW-COOKED GRITS
AND THE SWEET ICED TEA
WITH REFILLS FREE
AND CUPS OF JOE, AND COMPANY

THERE USED TO BE A SIGN UP
SAYING 'GLAD YOU CAME'
WHEN EV'RY LITTLE TOWN AROUND
WAS AS DIFF'RENT AS ITS NAME
NOW EVERYWHERE YOU GO
IT ALL JUST LOOKS THE SAME:

WALMART'S, WALGREENS
WENDY'S, APPLEBEES
STARBUCKS, STUCKEY'S
BEST BUY–

J.D., BENNY.

–MICKEY D'S.

BENNY.

AND THAT USED TO BE THE DRIVE IN
WHERE YOU TRIED TO MAKE SOME TIME

J.D.

AND THAT USED TO BE THE PHARMACY
NEXT TO WHAT USED TO BE THE 5 AND DIME

J.D. & BENNY.
 THEY SOLD ICES AT THE
  COUNTER
 LEMON, CHERRY, GRAPE OR
  LIME

J.D.
 THE CORNER STORE
 THE BARBER SHOP
 THE LIBRARY

BENNY.
 THE DRIVE IN
 THE MOM AND POP

BOTH.
 THE BAKERY.

J.D.
 NOW THIS TOWN'S JUST A COLLECTION
 OF SOME OLD GUY'S MEMORIES, JUST A

ALL.
 GHOST UPON A GHOST
 OF ALL THESE USED TO BE'S

J.D.
 BUT IF IT LOOKS THE SAME
 EVERYWHERE YOU ROAM
 TELL ME, HOW DO YOU KNOW
 WHEN YOU'VE GOTTEN HOME?

ALL.
 HOW DO YOU KNOW
 WHEN YOU'VE GOTTEN HOME?

J.D.
 ONE COFFEE CUP
 ONE K MART BRAND
 CHICKEN NUGGET SERVED
 THROUGHOUT THE LAND

NORMA.
 THE FRESH BREAD SMELL FROM THE BAKERY
 THAT USED TO FILL MY CAR

NORMA, KELLI, GREG, JESUS, HEATHER.
AAA-A-A-AHHHH
OOOOOOHHHH

J.D.
> THE LIGHTS FROM THE ALL NIGHT DINER
> SHINING LIKE MY TRUE NORTH STAR
> AND ALL THE

J.D., NORMA, BENNY.
> THOUSAND OTHER LITTLE THINGS

J.D.
> THAT MAKE US WHO WE ARE

KELLI, GREG.
> WALMARTS

BENNY.
> THE DRIVE IN

KELLI, GREG.
> WALGREENS

J.D.
> THE MOM AND POP

JESUS.
> WENDY'S

HEATHER.
> THE FIVE AND DIME

ALL.
> APPLEBEE'S

BENNY.
> STARBUCKS

J.D., NORMA.
> THE LIBRARIES

KELLI.
> SAM'S CLUB

J.D., JESUS.
> THE HOLLY TREES

GREG.
> DENNY'S

J.D.
> THE HONEY BEES

ALL.   **BENNY.**
> MICKEY D'S   MEMORIES

J.D.

ONLY MEMORIES

BENNY & J.D.

OF HOW WE USED TO BE.

NORMA.

WALMARTS, WALGREENS, WENDY'S.

(As the song ends, **JESUS***'s face brightens. He sees something that no one else does.)*

JESUS. *Hola perrita! Lolita, te dejaron sola todo el dia en la casa?*

(Everyone stares at **JESUS***, transfixed.)*

Viniste a darme animo, perrita?

HEATHER. What's he saying?

NORMA. *(concerned)* He's talking to his dog...

JESUS. *Te voy a dejar pasear en esta trocka, con tu narizita en el aire, y tus orejas volando.*

HEATHER. *(with dread)* I don't see a dog.

JESUS. *Donde encontraste eso?*

*(***JESUS*** removes his hand; everyone gasps.* **BENNY** *shakes his head with a world-weary cynicism.)*

*(***JESUS*** leans down and takes something from the illusory dog.)*

De quien es esa pelota de tenis?

BENNY. Happened back in ninety-four; Henry Snyder started talking to his dead wife.

NORMA. What'd she tell him?

BENNY. To let go.

JESUS. Okay, *Lolita. Preparate. Preparate para un batazo en el aire!*

*(***JESUS*** hurls the invisible ball in the air. He watches, gratified, as his "dog" gives chase.)*

Asi es perrita-asi es! Dale Lolita! Dale!

BENNY. Hey. Amigo. Looks like you're out.

*(***JESUS*** stares dully into the distance, then his face almost crumples in despair.)*

JESUS. I have to go home. I have to feed my dog. *(a beat)* I miss my dog.

(And he exits the lot.)

(His departure cuts through everyone like a cold wind. **BENNY** *glances toward the DJ's station.)*

BENNY. Where's that radio fella–?

J.D. Home. Sleepin'. *(wistfully)* On a mattress. Crisp cotton sheets.

(Without **FRANK** *to play the jingle,* **BENNY** *sings low.)*

BENNY.
FLOYD KING NISSAN
PICK UP AND–

*(***J.D.*** silences him with a look. An almost catatonic* **KELLI** *starts to sing a capella in a haunting key.)*

KELLI.
...GONE
SO FAR AWAY
GONE
LIKE YESTERDAY...

GREG. That's right, baby. He's gone.

*(***KELLI*** doesn't respond; she just keeps singing.)*

KELLI.
GONE
SO FAST SO FAR...

GREG. Kelli, don't do that.

KELLI.
GONE
LIKE A SHOOTING STAR...

*(***GREG*** grows alarmed)*

GREG. *(to the others)* –is she awake asleep?– *(back to* **KELLI***)* –Baby, wake up now.

KELLI.
GONE
LIKE ALL GOOD THINGS...

GREG. *(his anxiety growing)* You and me, and palm trees–

(KELLI turns to him in a trance-like state. He studies her face, but she looks past him, through him even, to some distant place.)

(a small voice) Don't. Please.

(But KELLI lifts her hand. GREG makes a futile gesture for her to stay, extending his arm and wiggling his fingers in an effort to roll back time, and will her to stay at the truck.)

(But in a slow, halting gait KELLI ventures into the night, following some remote point in the sky.)

(Perspiring, frantic, GREG asks the others.)

GREG. What do I do, huh?

NORMA. She's not right.

BENNY. You took a shine to her, didn't you?

GREG. Should I…

BENNY. That's up to you.

GREG. *(swallowing, hard)* Shit. Aw, shit. *(a pained beat)* She don't even have her shoes on. Nothing but slippers. *(looking after her)* We were gonna drive together. I…I was gonna be a stunt man.

BENNY. Where's she live?

GREG. Over near Jackson Park, she told me.

BENNY. Long way to walk home in her condition. Have to cross a freeway or two. Won't she J.D.?

(J.D. swallows, hard, but doesn't answer.)

BENNY. *(cont.)* Won't she?

J.D. *(capitulating)* West Marshall, turns into Highway 80.

BENNY. How many lanes is that? Norma? Two?

(NORMA pauses, wracked with guilt.)

NORMA. Four. I think it's four.

BENNY. What time's rush hour start? Heather, you know?

HEATHER. Rush hour? *(in a tiny voice)* 'Bout now, I guess.

BENNY. Son, I hope and pray that poor girl still has sense enough to look both ways 'fore crossing the street.

(**GREG** *looks at his own hand, anchored to the truck. He looks after* **KELLI**. *Back at his hand. Back in the direction of* **KELLI**.)

GREG. How much you figure they cost, plane tickets to Los Angeles? *(a hoarse whisper) Holy shit.*

*(the sound of morning traffic, and the strains of **I'M GONE**)*

Fuck it.

(**GREG** *lets go and rushes out, calling as he goes*)

Kelli. *KELLI–*

(And he's gone, too. The **OTHERS** *stand, profoundly uneasy with themselves.* **NORMA** *is near tears.)*

NORMA. May God forgive me.

(Even **BENNY**'s *a little shaken by what he's just done.)*

BENNY. Cruel game, people. Damn cruel game.

(Time passes; it's lunch time on the fourth day.)

(Inside the dealership, **MIKE** *is on the phone. He starts out convivial, even light-hearted.)*

MIKE. …I was a kid, I'd say, "I'd like three drumsticks," and my Mama, she'd say, "A turkey only has two. Your eyes are bigger than your stomach, baby." So you see, Dan… *(clearing his throat)* …it's always been kind of a problem with me…

(He attempts a casual laugh. It comes out strained.)

MIKE. A candy store? No! Just a few extra vehicles is all. But I'll cold canvas, forfeit my spiffs, whatever it takes… *(suddenly he turns belligerent)* Damn right Tyler's got better figures. It's a BIGGER CITY. You pay an on-site visit once in a blue moon, you'd know…

(His tone changes; now it's confidential, even contrite.)

MIKE. Look, my wife Stacey and me, we're over-extended. She wants this Tuscan marble, for Chrissakes. I got this asshole loan officer sending me certified letters– *(a whisper now)* –I'm no good, Dan, and she knows it. This new kitchen, I was tryin' to make things right– *(a beat)* Dan?

(Outside at the truck, the sun crests at mid-afternoon.)

*(**HEATHER** whispers to **NORMA**.)*

HEATHER. These gloves are 'sposed to be cotton, aren't they?

NORMA. That's what the lady said.

HEATHER. Cotton don't bother me, but *this glove...*you think it's a poly-blend?

NORMA. It's scratchy, all right.

HEATHER. Feels like somebody poured ground glass into it!

NORMA. Last break, I put some lotion on; that helped a little.

*(**HEATHER**'s whole body shivers.)*

HEATHER. Oh, God, help me! It's making me crazy.

NORMA. Don't think about it; that just makes it worse–

HEATHER. –but it's itchin' so bad– *(trying to distract herself) Puppies and rainbows! Puppies and rainbows! Puppies and rainbows! (in agony)* It's not working! Nothing's working!

NORMA. *(squirming)* Now you got me thinking about it, too.

HEATHER. I try thinking about NOT thinking about it, but it doesn't help...

BENNY. Mine's downright comfy.

*(**BENNY** drums his fingers on the surface of the car.)*

Like silk. Like a second skin.

*(**HEATHER** becomes increasingly agitated. Her shoulders twitch.)*

HEATHER. Well, mine *hurts*, mine *hurts*, mine *hurts, mine hurts!*

(**BENNY** *turns to* **J.D.** *and says in a low voice*)

BENNY. Adderal? Dexedrine? What you wager?

J.D. You serious?

BENNY. Look at her. She's shaking like a dog tryin' to piss a peach pit.

J.D. That'd be a violation, wouldn't it?

BENNY. So? 'Bout four years ago, man named Dirk Scobie took hisself some speed. Wanted to quit, but his hand went to sleep. Couldn't lift it off the bumper, *dead weight.* Started to bite it instead, like a bear caught in a trap, chewin' off its own claw–

HEATHER. *Ow! Ow! Ow! Ow!*

BENNY. Wound up at the State Hospital over in Terrell.

HEATHER. *(increasingly hysterical)* Screw this. I can't take this–*I can't–*

BENNY. Maximum security ward.

HEATHER. *(calling)* Mr. Ferris! Mr. Ferris–

(**CINDY** *comes out of the dealership.*)

CINDY. What do you want?

HEATHER. Can I talk to Mike?

CINDY. He's on a cot back there, sleeping.

HEATHER. Would you mind waking him up?

CINDY. Yes. I'd very much mind. I'm not gonnna do that; now can I help you?

HEATHER. *Mr. Ferris will understand.*

CINDY. Whatever Mike understands, I understand, too.

HEATHER. I need another glove; this one's giving me hives.

CINDY. Nothing wrong with these gloves; we use the same brand every year–

HEATHER. *(sputtering tears) Please, please, please!* I want a different one–

CINDY. No can do. That's "preferential treatment."

(**HEATHER** *realizes that it's a losing battle with* **CINDY**)

HEATHER. *(shouting again)* Mike! MIKE!

CINDY. Hush up, that's enough.

HEATHER. *MIIIIIIIKE!*

(*A disheveled* MIKE *steps out.*)

MIKE. Huh? What is it? What's going on?

HEATHER. (*wild-eyed now*) I'm taking off this stupid glove—

CINDY. You can't do that! (*to* MIKE) She cannot do that! (*back to* HEATHER) You know the rules. Gloves must be worn at all times—

MIKE. —she's right—

CINDY. —nobody wants to win a truck that's got a hand print in the paint finish—

HEATHER. *I'm not making this up; you think I am but I'm not—*

MIKE. (*desperate*) Hold on. I know. What say you swap out your glove for a new one at the next break—

BENNY. (*big protest*) Whoa, whoa, whoa—

CINDY. (*to* MIKE) They'd all hafta agree—

MIKE. —sure; why won't they—

HEATHER. Nobody's gonna agree—they'd sooner stab me and watch me die—

CINDY. Then I'm sorry, Heather, but there's nothing we can do. (*sternly*) *Tell her, Mike.*

MIKE. (*protesting to* CINDY) But she—

(CINDY*'s glare silences him. He turns to* HEATHER:)

(*in a corner*) She...ah...she's right. There's no favoritism.

HEATHER. Yes! Yes, there is! *And you should be favoring me, but you're not!*

(*SONG:* ***IT'S A FIX (REPRISE)***)

CINDY. "Hari kari," Mike. That's what it's called.

MIKE. (*to* HEATHER) The heat fried your brain, or what?

HEATHER. You know damn well we had a deal!

FRANK. Seems we've encountered controversy here at the Hands on a Hardbody—

(MIKE *rips the cord out of* FRANK*'s mike.*)

Jesus, Mike!

MIKE. *(to* **HEATHER***)* Get the hell off my lot—

> *(But* **HEATHER** *turns to rally her fellow* **CONTESTANTS,** *who are agape.)*

HEATHER. *(sings)*
> HE TOOK ME TO DINNER
> SAID YOU'LL BE OUR WINNER
> I PROMISE THAT WE'LL TREAT YOU RIGHT
> YOU'LL POSE BY THE TIRES
> WE'LL GET THE RIGHT BUYERS
> YOU'RE PRETTY, YOU'RE YOUNG AND YOU'RE WHITE.
>
> YOU GOT TO BELIEVE THIS
> THEY WEREN'T GOING TO LEAVE THIS
> TO CHANCE, AIN'T NO CHANCE THAT YOU'D WIN.
> IT AIN'T WHO'S THE STRONGEST
> OR WHO'LL LAST THE LONGEST
> YOU WERE ALL SCREWED GOIN IN!
>
> THE FIBER'S EATEN CLEAR THROUGH MY SKIN
> YOU PROMISED ME THAT YOU'D LET ME WIN
> AND NOW YOU'RE HERE PRETENDIN'
> YOU LOVE HICKS AND SPOOKS AND SPICS!
> OH, IT'S A FIX!
> IT'S A FIX!

> *(***HEATHER** *yanks her hand off the truck. She rips off the gloves. She shakes her hand out, furiously, like it's on fire.)*

> *(***MIKE** *grabs her by the arm. As he drags her off, she gives a sharp cry.)*

> *(***FRANK** *does the usual.)*

JINGLE.

> *FLOYD KING NISSAN*

> *PICK UP AND GO!*

FRANK. Ms. Heather Stovall, off in a blaze of intrigue.

> *(***CINDY** *finds herself alone with he* **CONTESTANTS***. They aim their eyes at her like gun barrels.)*

CINDY. *(eager to leave)* Next break's in twenty minutes–

J.D. Ms. Barnes?

CINDY. Yes?

J.D. You gonna run a clean contest now?

BENNY. That girl was more jacked up than an antique Chevy on a redneck's lawn.

*(**CINDY**' face turns a hot red.)*

CINDY. I'll have you know I am a member in good standing of the National Automobile Dealers Association. I signed a pledge, and that pledge hangs over my desk, in a gold frame, next to snapshots of my two baby girls. In it, I promise to display the very highest standards of ethical conduct. I intend to uphold it, even if others do not.

*(With that, she marches into the office. She gives **MIKE** a withering look.)*

A samurai sword. Left to right, in the gut, same way you'd clean a deer.

*(**MIKE** has nothing to say. Meanwhile, outside:)*

J.D. First time in four days, the playin' field is even.

*(**RONALD** enters, revitalized.)*

BENNY. Well, look who's here. I'd a thought this was the last place you'd wanna be.

RONALD. Hate this place; can't stand this place. I said to myself, "If I never see this place again, that is too soon for me!" But see...I got this problem. I was home with my lady friend, she talkin' a blue-streak, but I got this glaze on me. Finally she said, "You here, baby, but your heart, it's someplace else." She was thinkin' it was with Peaches or Shana Charisse, but it wasn't. It was right here at this truck, next to Ms. Valverde.

NORMA. *(a little delirious)* Larry! You came back!

RONALD. I'm Ronald; Ronald McCowan.

NORMA. *(to **BENNY**)* He's a good man, I told you. He came back! *(back to **RONALD**)* How long...

RONALD. Dropped off three days ago. Three whole days! But look at you! Still holding strong. Final three!

NORMA. Lord shows me strength I didn't know I had.

RONALD. He sure does. *(with even more oomph) You in the final three!*

(Still smarting from before, **CINDY** *enters to do damage control.)*

CINDY. Okay, people! We gotta ensure– *(clearing her throat)* –for fairness– *(blushing a bit)* –nobody's been using artificial stimulants to stay awake. So we're givin' each one of you a drug test–

BENNY. *(amused)* She for real?

CINDY. –all you gotta do is pee in a cup. *(brandishing them in her hand)* I got these little dipsticks right here. Yours turns red, you're out. Now I'm gonna take you inside one person at a time, and it's gonna count as your break. Mr. Drew?

J.D. Yes, mam.

*(***CINDY*** escorts ***J.D.*** into the dealership. ***NORMA*** shifts her weight back and forth.)*

NORMA. *(almost robotic) Bao diddy bao diddy bao bao bao...Bao diddy bao diddy bao bao bao... (then sadly)* Talk to me, Ronald, because my mind's gone.

RONALD. You just gotta stand tight. I noticed you was getting closer and closer to the truck. You don't wanna be doin' that; looks like you're leanin'. You can't lean–

NORMA. *(a mantra)* Can't lean, can't lean, can't lean.

RONALD. You want a cold rag on your head? I can get you a cold rag.

NORMA. *(suddenly lost)* Where are we? What am I doin' here?

RONALD. You in the contest. You gonna win this truck.

NORMA. *(nodding)* That's right. I came for this truck. This truck, this truck.

*(***BENNY*** can't help but overhear their conversation)*

RONALD. First day, I seen that J.D. fella drive up in four wheels he's already got. A Buick! He don't need no truck.

NORMA. *(nodding, rote)* No truck, no truck, no truck.

RONALD. *(nodding toward* **BENNY***)* And that other one. Look at him down there, all by his lonesome. Folks cheerin' you, Norma. Nobody cheerin' him.

BENNY. Ain't that sweet. You the wind beneath her wings, ain't ya?

RONALD. Where your friends at?

BENNY. Sorry, Casanova, she's married lady–

RONALD. Where's your family?

BENNY. *Family?* You're her family now?

RONALD. Nobody bringin' *you* sweet tea–

BENNY. Shit, man, you've known her–what?–three days–

RONALD. Ain't nobody rubbin' *your* feet.

BENNY. I'm doin' fine.

RONALD. You got yourself a lady, where's she?

BENNY. *(darkening)* Hey.

RONALD. That son you brag about, where's he?

BENNY. Hey, HEY.

RONALD. Big Marine, too high up for his Daddy?

BENNY. Shut your damn mouth.

RONALD. They gone, ain't they? Man reaps what he sows, and they gone–

BENNY. –you heard me–

RONALD. –all gone–

BENNY. –*shut it NOW*–

RONALD. –what you do? Drive 'em all away?–

BENNY. –I'll *take* you–

RONALD. –winning this truck ain't gonna bring 'em back–

BENNY. –*you want me to take you*–?

> *(***BENNY*** surges forward to attack, but it's impossible for him to reach* **RONALD** *with disengaging from the truck. He's like an angry dog, straining at the end of its leash.)*

RONALD. Careful. Don't be taking your hand off.

(As BENNY smolders, RONALD says with lacerating clarity.)

You win, what happens? You gonna park it in your yard. You gonna stare at it through a dirty window, all by yourself in an empty house. Oh, you a big man all right. You a "champion."

(This hits BENNY hard, but he doesn't say anything. RONALD focuses on NORMA again.)

RONALD. But you? You win, what you gonna do?

NORMA. Drive my babies to school.

RONALD. That's right!

NORMA. Drive my husband to a new job.

RONALD. The future, not the past!

NORMA. Drive us all to the Lord's house on Sunday.

RONALD. Amen! You win, you make the world a better place.

NORMA. Better.

RONALD. You got a prayer chain so big, it circles twice around the world.

(NORMA answers with a trace of her old spirit.)

NORMA. Hallelujah.

RONALD. (with a glance at BENNY) I don't wanna live in a world where a man like him can take home the prize. (back to NORMA) You win it for all of us, all right?

(She nods, fiercely.)

You want your music? You want your music now?

(NORMA nods again. RONALD places the earphones from her mp3 player on her head. She bops up and down gently as the music courses through her.)

(J.D. re-enters, CINDY on his heels).

CINDY. Next up, Ms. Valverde.

(NORMA doesn't hear)

MS. VALVERDE.

*(**RONALD** gestures to her)*

NORMA. Oh!

*(**NORMA** removes her earphones, then follows **CINDY**)*

BENNY. *(stopping her)* Yo, Norma. You talk to God a helluva lot. He ever... *(a vulnerable hitch in his throat)* ...he ever talk back?

*(**NORMA** gives him a curious look, then heads inside. **RONALD** follows her. **J.D.** resumes his place at the truck.)*

*(Suddenly, **BENNY** lurches forward, drawing a sharp intake of breath.)*

BENNY. *(cont.)* Shit.

J.D. What is it, Benny? What's wrong?

BENNY. I'm numb.

*(color drains from **J.D.**'s face)*

Started in my feet 'bout two hours ago. Went up through my calves, over my knees, like the Good Lord drew me on a piece of paper then decided to erase what he'd done from the bottom up...

J.D. Well, shake it out–

BENNY. Can't feel what to shake.

J.D. Then say it. Say it.

BENNY. No can do, amigo.

J.D. One more time. Just say it. "Cuervo."

BENNY. *(flaring up insistently)* What'd I tell you? When I was talking about going numb, what did I say? *What did I say?*

J.D. That it's too late.

BENNY. What you look so blue for? You're playing *against* me, not with me–

J.D. *–I know that!–*

BENNY. *(with gravity) Don't you wanna win?*

J.D. Don't you?

BENNY. You win, someone's got to lose.

J.D. That's not you talkin, friend.

    *(SONG: **GOD ANSWERED MY PRAYERS**)*

BENNY. Oh, I hoped to win; prayed to win. Hell, even Benny prays. Me and the Lord, we go way back.

    (sings)

I ASKED HIM FOR A WINDFALL
TO LIFT ME FROM THIS HOLE
I ASKED HIM FOR A WOMAN
TO ROCK ME TO MY SOUL
'LET US MAKE LOVE IN THE SAND
LET THAT GOOD TEQUILA FLOW.'
GOD ANSWERED MY PRAYERS
–HE SAID 'NO.'

I SAID, PLEASE REMOVE MY NEIGHBORS
CAN'T YOU SEE THEY'RE MEXICAN?
THEY DON'T EVEN SHARE OUR LANGUAGE
OR THE COLOR OF OUR SKIN
THEY JUST SNUCK INTO OUR COUNTRY
OH LORD, WON'T YOU MAKE 'EM GO?
GOD ANSWERED MY PRAYERS
HE SAID, 'NO.'

THERE ISN'T ANY TIME OF DAY
THAT YOU DON'T HAVE HIS EAR
BUT HE MAY NOT GIVE YOU THE ANSWER
THAT YOU WANT TO HEAR.
HE HOLDS US IN HIS PERFECT LOVE
HE'S THERE FOR EVERYONE
SO DON'T YOU BLAME HIM
FOR YOUR SORROWS
BETTER LOOK AT WHAT YOU'VE DONE

I SAID 'STOP HER LORD'
MY WIFE WAS WALKING OUT THE DOOR.
I SAID 'SPARE HIM LORD'
MY CHILD FLEW OFF TO WAR.
AND I KNOW THAT HE WAS LISTENING
'CAUSE I FELT A CHILL WIND BLOW
GOD ANSWERED MY PRAYERS

BENNY.   **BACKUPS.**

    HE SAID, 'NO.'   WHOAAAA, WHOAAA...

BENNY. His third deployment. My son started havin' nightmares, cryin' out in his sleep, scarin' the hell outta his bunk mates. Uncle Sam gave him an honorable discharge. Got his old room ready; wrote "welcome home" in shoe polish on my front window. *(a beat)* Night before his transfer, he took his M-9, turned it on hisself.

J.D. I'm real sorry Benny.

BENNY.   **BACKUPS.**

YOU NEVER HAVE TO BE ALONE	
HE'S ALWAYS BY YOUR SIDE	
BUT YOU KNOW YOU BETTER	
KNEEL DOWN BEFORE HIM	KNEEL DOWN BEFORE HIM
OR YOU'LL DROWN IN YOUR OWN PRIDE	DROWN IN YOUR OWN PRIDE
YOU ALWAYS GOT TO RUN THE SHOW	
YOU THINK YOU'RE IN YOUR CONTROL	
AND YOU'RE HELL-BENT FOR GLORY	HELL-BENT FOR GLORY
AT THE COST OF YOUR OWN SOUL	COST OF YOUR OWN SOUL
	OOOOOOOOOHH
I SAID HELP ME LORD	AAAAAHHHH
WON'T YOU SHOW ME WHAT TO DO?	AAAAHHHH
DON'T FORSAKE ME LORD	
THE WAY I'VE FORSAKEN YOU	AAAAHHHH
I'M TIRED AND I'M BROKEN	OOOOOHHHH
AND I'M SCARED OF LETTING GO	AAAAHHHHH

(Feverish and spent, **BENNY** *hears the phantom voices of other* **CONTESTANTS,** *past and present:* **NORMA, CHRIS, JESUS, HEATHER, KELLI, GREG,** *etc.)*

NORMA.	**OTHERS.**
WHOAAA *(improv)*	OH, OH, OH, OH
	OH, OH, OH, OH
	OH, OH, OH, OH
	OH, OH, OH, OH
	AAAAHHH, AAAAHHH
	AAAAHHH, AAAAHHH
	MMMMMM

*(***BENNY*** falls to his knees)*

BENNY.

O LORD, I KNEEL BEFORE YOU HERE
ON THE EDGE OF THIS ABYSS.
I BEG YOU TO RELEASE ME
FROM MY FOOLISH RIGHTEOUSNESS
AND MY POISON PREJUDICE
AND THIS AWFUL EMPTINESS.

GOD ANSWERED MY PRAYERS.
HE SAID, 'YES.'

(released of his demons, **BENNY** *lets go of the truck)*

*(***CINDY*** enters with* **NORMA,** *who walks stoically toward the truck and places her hand on the hood.* **RONALD** *follows.)*

CINDY. Benny? Benny Perkins?

*(***BENNY*** gives a rueful little laugh)*

BENNY. It's done. This thing's done.

(With all his might, **BENNY** *strives to walk, to move one foot in front of the other. He can't. His feet are rooted to the ground, immobile. He's lost all sensation. In frustration, he gives a strong shove with his hands, loses his balance, and collapses onto the groundd.)*

(Unexpectedly, **CHRIS** *shouts from the shadows.)*

CHRIS. Someone give him a hand!

JINGLE.

FLOYD KING NISSAN

PICK UP AND GO

(**FRANK** *and* **CINDY** *gingerly lift* **BENNY** *off the ground.*)

FRANK. Ladies and gentlemen, the champion Benny Perkins, down.

(**BENNY** *catches sight of* **CHRIS** *lurking in the shadows*)

BENNY. How long you been there, son?

(**CHRIS** *turns abruptly to leave, then stops. Instead, he steps forward.*)

You fell off days ago. Ain't you got no place to go?

(*Impulsively,* **CHRIS** *moves toward* **BENNY** *to speak confidentially.*)

CHRIS. I promised my wife...my boy...I promised my son I'd be driving home in a big red truck. He thinks I'm still in the game. Minute he sees me walkin' up the driveway, he'll know... (*a beat*) I trained with your son over at Pendleton.

BENNY. 'S that so?

CHRIS. He was a good marine. He was. I never meant to suggest otherwise. He had a lotta bad thoughts, that's all. He just wanted 'em to end. (*a beat*) I do, too, sometimes.

BENNY. You made it home, son. So you hold on.

CHRIS. I'll try, sir.

(*with* **CHRIS**'*s support,* **BENNY** *slowly, fitfully starts ambling off the lot.*)

RONALD. Mr. Perkins?

(**BENNY** *stops and turns to regard* **RONALD.**)

You take care now.

(**BENNY** *gives him a grateful nod. As he exits, he passes his sunglasses to* **J.D.** *With his final look,* **BENNY** *practically wills* **J.D.** *to win.*)

(Then **BENNY***'s gone.* **CHRIS** *lingers behind. Day shifts into night.)*

(Only two **CONTESTANTS** *at the truck;* **NORMA**, *moving in slow rhythm to the sounds on her mp3 player. And* **J.D.**, *implacable as ever.)*

FRANK. Tomorrow will mark day five, people. Day Five. I'm here with J.D. Drew, one of only two competitors still standing here at Floyd King Nissan. *(holding his mike to* **J.D.***)* Did you expect to make final two, J.D.?

J.D. I expect to win.

FRANK. What's your secret?

J.D. Benny Perkins. I'm gonna have to honestly say that. *(fondly)* You listenin', Benny? I hope you are. Cuz my place on this truck, I owe it to you, my brother.

FRANK. And Ms. Norma Valverde–

*(***FRANK** *notices that* **NORMA** *is in her own world, between earphones)*

–Ms. Valverde? Hello?

(But she's oblivious, so he seeks out **RONALD** *instead.)*

Mr. McCowan, are you surprised to see Norma still here?

RONALD. No, on accounta people underestimate Norma. Age-wise, she's in the middle. And she's a full-figured woman, too, carries it real well–

FRANK. But health-wise…?

RONALD. A liability, no question. But you know why she's gonna drive home in that truck today?

FRANK. Why?

RONALD. Because she's enlisted her Higher Pow–

*(***RONALD***'s distracted by a clicking sound. He looks over to see* **NORMA**, *frantically pushing the buttons on her mp3 player. She looks up, meeting* **RONALD***'s gaze.)*

NORMA. He's gone dead.

RONALD. What's the matter?

NORMA. *(dismayed) He's gone dead on me.*

RONALD. Your battery?

NORMA. He said he'd sing to me. He said he'd lift me up–

RONALD. Honey, you just ran outta juice. I got a charger in my car–

NORMA. No; you don't understand.

RONALD. You're wore out, that's all.

NORMA. *He's abandoned me–*

RONALD. You lost your horse sense–

NORMA. The Bible says honor thy Holy Father and He will provide–

RONALD. He will; you know He will–

NORMA. *(near tears) Why would He forsake me now? Why? I've done everything He told me to do?*

(In a quiet voice, **RONALD** *starts to substitute* **NORMA***'s taped songs with live music instead.)*

*(SONG: **THE JOY OF THE LORD (REPRISE)**)*

RONALD. *(quietly)*
I FEEL THE JOY
I FEEL THE JOY
I FEEL THE JOY IN ME
LIFTING MY PAIN
WHEN I NEED IT TO BE

(a beat)

NORMA. He's gone. He's not here. Not for me.

(Exhaustion overtakes **NORMA**, *and she can't hold back the tears. Silence, then:)*

RONALD.
WHO WHO WHO?
HAPPY IS HE HE HE
HAPPY AM I I I
HAPPY ARE WE WE WE

(to **CHRIS***)*

HAPPY IS WHO WHO WHO?

*(**RONALD** prods **CHRIS** to join him.)*

CHRIS.
HAPPY IS HE HE HE
RONALD & CHRIS.
HAPPY AM I I I
HAPPY ARE WE WE WE WE

RONALD.	**CHRIS.**
KEEP ON BELIEVING	WHO WHO WHO
LIKE YOU ALWAYS DO	HAPPY IS HE HE HE
CAUSE I FEEL THE LORD HERE	HAPPY AM I I I
IS WORKING THROUGH YOU	HAPPY ARE WE WE WE
HOW CAN YOU TELL ME	HAPPY IS WHO WHO WHO
THAT HE ISN'T NEAR	HAPPY IS HE HE HE
WHEN YOU'VE BROUGHT HIS SPIRIT	HAPPY AM I I I
TO EVERYONE HERE?	HAPPY ARE WE WE WE
DO YOU FEEL HIS HOLY JOY?	

RONALD & CHRIS.
YES!

CHRIS. *(to **RONALD**)*
WOO! DO YOU FEEL HIS HOLY JOY?

RONALD & CHRIS.
YE-EA-EA-ESS!
DOES HE BLESS THIS LADY WITH HIS HOLINESS?
IS GOD WATCHING OVER HER?

*(A beat, and **NORMA** is convinced.)*

NORMA. *(smiles)*
YES.

*(**NORMA** sings; the **OTHERS** sing and clap along)*

NORMA.	**RONALD, CHRIS.**
I FEEL THE JOY!	
	I FEEL THE JOY!
I FEEL IT E-VE-RY-DAY!	

I FEEL THE JOY!

AND WHEN I LAUGH WITH
   THE LORD!

I FEEL THE JOY!

HE TAKES MY PAIN A-WAY!

I FEEL THE JOY!

I AIN'T TIRED NO MORE!

I FEEL THE JOY!

I AIN'T NO WAY SORE!

I FEEL THE JOY!

THE DEVIL WILL NEVER
   DEVIL

I FEEL THE JOY!

NORMA NO MORE!

NORMA NO MORE!

NORMA NO MORE!

NORMA NO MORE!

NORMA NO MORE!

NORMA NO MORE!

THE DEVIL WILL NEVER
   DEVIL

ALL.

NORMA NO MORE!

NORMA.   **RONALD, CHRIS.**

I FEEL THE JOY!

I AIN'T RIED NO MORE!

I FEEL THE JOY!

I AIN'T NO WAY SORE!

I FEEL THE JOY!

THE DEVIL WILL NEVER
   DEVIL
NOR-MA...

(Moved by the spirit of the Lord and the compassion demonstrated by her friends, **NORMA** *begins to clap too. Joyously. Unfettered.)*

*(***NORMA** *looks down at her clapping hands, as if they're moving of their own free will.* **EVERYONE** *stares.)*

NORMA.

NO...

(**NORMA** *realizes what she's done.*)

...MORE.

(**NORMA**'s *face slackens, her knees buckle, and she passes out.*)

(**CHRIS** *and* **RONALD** *grab her in the nick of time, before she falls.*)

J.D. What just happened? Somebody, tell me. *(in a daze)* Somebody, please...

RONALD. She got happy with the Lord, that's what. She got happy.

(**CHRIS** *kneels down and mops* **NORMA**'s *face with paper towels.*)

CHRIS. Sorry, mam. Real sorry.

RONALD. You wanna go inside and cool off?

NORMA. Where's my husband? Where's Ramon?

RONALD. With your kids. He's with your kids. You wanna sit in the air conditioning?

NORMA. I want to go home. That's all I want. *(in a small voice) Won't someone please take me home?*

(**CHRIS** *and* **RONALD** *hold her up as she takes painful, halting steps off the concrete.*)

(**J.D.** *is alone at the truck. The contest feels a million miles away; there's only the void of night, and a lone man, standing astride a truck, his hand planted on it, teetering gently in the breeze like some oracular figure from a long lost Beckett play.*)

(**J.D.**'s *wife* **VIRGINIA** *returns, a basket of provisions for him in hand.*)

(**J.D.** *sees her.*)

J.D. *(choked up)* Virginia?

VIRGINIA. Had the radio on, to keep me company. They said you was close to winning.

J.D. You been followin' this thing?

VIRGINIA. What'm I 'sposed to do?

(**VIRGINIA** *gives a slight, ironic smile.*)

Sit at home all day by myself? You know how much I hate that.

(**J.D.** *gets it and grins.*)

VIRGINIA. *(cont.)* J.D. Where'd everybody go?

J.D. They're gone, ain't they? All gone but me.

VIRGINIA. Don't that mean…? Aren't you…?

(**J.D.** *cries out to nobody in particular, almost plaintively.*)

J.D. Last man standing, right? *(a beat)* Can I do it? Can I take my hand off?

(**FRANK** *bolts forward to announce the obvious.*)

FRANK. *That's a new world's record, people! Ninety-one hours, sixteen minutes, and twenty-seven seconds!* And the proud winner, Mr. J.D. Drew!

(*Slowly, painfully,* **J.D.** *raises his hands from the truck. Then he turns to* **VIRGINIA**.)

J.D. What you think, baby?

VIRGINIA. Careful, you.

FRANK. J.D., my man. How's it feel?

(*SONG: **KEEP YOUR HANDS ON IT**)*

J.D. *(sings)*
I HAVE NEVER BEEN THE KIND OF GUY
WHO PUT HIS FAITH IN LUCK
I WAS STUBBORN, I WAS PATIENT
I WOULDN'T LEAVE WITHOUT THIS TRUCK!

MY DADDY ALWAYS TOLD ME,
DON'T WAIT FOR YOUR LUCKY SHIP
YOU CAN NAB IT
GO AND GRAB IT
JUST DON'T EVER LOSE YOUR GRIP.

IF YOU WANT SOMETHING
KEEP YOUR HANDS ON IT
HOLD IT CLOSE TO YOU
DON'T LET GO ONE BIT
COULD BE SOMEONE ELSE
MAY HAVE PLANS ON IT
SO IF YOU WANT SOMETHING...
KEEP YOUR HANDS ON IT
JUST KEEP YOUR HANDS ON IT.

   *(**MIKE** and **CINDY** come out of the dealership. **MIKE** hands **J.D.** the keys to the truck.)*

MIKE. Congratulations, friend.

   *(**MIKE** and **J.D.** pose for a picture.)*

CINDY. Smile!

   *(**J.D.** takes **VIRGINIA**'s hand, and presses the keys into her palm. She looks at him in shock.)*

VIRGINIA. What are you giving these to me for?

J.D. I won it for you. Whatsa matter, don't you want it? Got a bench seat, just the way you like.

   *(**VIRGINIA** beams through tears.)*

FROM THE MOMENT I FIRST SAW YOU
I KNEW I HAD TO MAKE YOU MINE
THERE WERE OTHER GUYS WITH HUNGRY EYES
JUST WAITIN' IN A LINE
I GRABBED YOU AND I HELD YOU CLOSE
FIRST CHANCE I COULD GET
CHILLS WENT THROUGH ME
HUGGED YOU TO ME
AND I HAVEN'T LET GO YET

IF YOU WANT SOMETHING
KEEP YOUR HANDS ON IT
CLING WITH ALL YOUR SOUL
WHEN YOU FIND YOUR FIT

VIRGINIA.

IT MAY BREAK YOUR HEART
IT MAY HURT A BIT
BUT IF YOU LOVE SOMETHING
KEEP YOUR HANDS ON IT.

J.D. & VIRGINIA.

IF YOU LOVE SOMETHING
KEEP YOUR HANDS ON IT.

(**J.D.** *opens the truck door for* **VIRGINIA** *with all the tenderness a newlywed might demonstrate when opening the door to a first home.*)

CINDY. I almost wanna cry.

MIKE. I'll give you something to cry about; Tennessee says we've got sixty days. First thing tomorrow? Liquidation sale.

(**CINDY** *stares at him, eviscerated.*)

FRANK. Next week we'll be broadcasting live from the Cajun Chili Cook-off; my wife Arlene's got a recipe for armadillo that's worth a notch on your belt, trust me. This is Frank Nugent, KYKX, with a special thanks to all our contestants.

(*The* **CONTESTANTS** *all converge onstage, ready to disclose their various fates.*)

CHRIS.

WATCHED MY SON HIT HIS FIRST SINGLE
AT HIS FIRST TIME UP AT BAT
HAD A PART TIME JOB AND LOST IT
I'M STILL NOT SO GOOD AT THAT
MY WIFE AND I ARE TALKING MORE

CHRIS & JESUS.

WE'LL HAVE TO WAIT AND SEE

JESUS.

I'M STILL WORKING DOUBLE SHIFTS
I'M GONNA GET THAT DAMN DEGREE.

RONALD.

> MY LADY FRIEND GOT ME THIS JOB
> HER DADDY FIXES HIGHWAY LIGHTS
> SO I'M ALL SET–NO PROBLEM
> PROBLEM IS–I'M SCARED OF HEIGHTS!

JANIS.

> WHILE THE WORLD REWARDS THE CHEATERS
> WE AIN'T GOT TWO CENTS TO SPARE

DON.

> GOT OUR FAMILY

JANIS.

> GOT EACH OTHER

DON & JANIS.

> AND OUR TWENTY TONS OF AIR!

CHRIS, JESUS, FRANK, RONALD, DON, JANIS.

> IF YOU WANT SOMETHING
> KEEP YOUR HANDS ON IT
> LET THEM TAKE YOUR PRIDE
> IT WON'T HURT A BIT

ALL. (*except* **BENNY, NORMA, CINDY, MIKE, VIRGINIA, J.D.**)

> AND IF YOU LOVE SOMEONE
> KEEP YOUR HANDS ON THEM
> LET THEM TAKE YOUR HEART
> IT BELONGS TO THEM

KELLI.

> NO, I DIDN'T WIN THE CONTEST
> IT'S TURNED OUT OKAY I GUESS

GREG.

> GOT HER SAFELY HOME THAT NIGHT

KELLI.

> GOT HIM A JOB AT UPS

BOTH.

> WE'RE SAVING REALLY CAREFUL
> EACH WEEK STASHING SOME AWAY
> FOR THE BIG TWO-WEEK VACATION HITTIN' VEGAS AND LA!
> FROM THE 28TH UNTIL THE 12TH OF MAY–WE'RE GONE!

NORMA.

RAMON'S STILL IN SEARCH OF STEADY WORK
OURS NOT TO QUESTION WHY
I GOT EXTRA HOURS AT MY JOB, WITH GOD'S HELP–WE GET
    BY
NOW I SEE HE DIDN'T BRING ME
TO THIS CONTEST ON A WHIM
HE PUT ME IN IT, NOT TO WIN IT,
BUT TO BRING MORE SOULS TO HIM

CINDY.

FLOYD KING NISSAN, IT WENT BELLY UP
WE COULDN'T FILL THE QUOTA

MIKE.

BUT THE CONTEST STILL CONTINUES

CINDY AND **MIKE.**

RIGHT HERE AT FLOYD KING TOYOTA!

HEATHER.

I ENTERED IT AGAIN NEXT YEAR
I NEVER THOUGHT I'D DARE!
BUT I DONE IT
AND I WON IT!
ONLY THIS TIME FAIR AND SQUARE!

*(***HEATHER*** gives the audience a telling wink.)*

ALL. *(no* **BENNY***)*

IF YOU WANT SOMETHING
LET YOUR PURPOSE SHOW
HOLD IT CLOSE TO YOU
DON'T YOU LET IT GO

LET IT BE YOUR GUIDE
STAR OF BETHLEHEM
IF YOU WANT SOMETHING…
DON'T LET GO

*(***BENNY*** enters for the final time.)*

DON'T LET GO

BENNY. Me, I'm doing fine.

ALL.
DON'T LET GO

BENNY. Sleeping over my Mama's garage, til things even out.

ALL.
OOOOOOOOOOO....

BENNY. *(spoken)* DON'T THINK THE CONTEST'S OVER

BENNY. *(spoken)*	**ALL.** *(no* **BENNY***)*
JUST CAUSE THE TENT IS GONE	
THIS CONTEST IS FOR LIFE, ANDIT GOES ON AND ON AND ON.	OOOOOOOOOOOO...
WE'RE ALL AROUND THE TRUCK HERE, THE BEST SOULS AND THE WORST.	OOOOOOOOOOOO...
SLACK-JAWED WITH EXCITEMENT JUST TO SEE WHO'LL DROP OFF FIRST	OOOOOOOOOOOO...
THAT'S THE NATURE OF US CREATURES LIVING ON THIS PLANET EARTH.	OOOOOOOOOOOO...
YOU'RE FIGHTING FOR YOUR BREATH RIGHT FROM THE MOMENT OF YOUR BIRTH!	OOOOOOOOOOOO...
(sings) SO IF YOU WANT SOMETHING KEEP YOUR HANDS ON IT	
	DON'T LET GO!
AND IF YOU LOVE SOMEONE KEEP YOUR HANDS ON THEM	

DON'T LET GO!

IF YOU LOSE
     EVERYTHING...

AAAAAAHHHH

BENNY & ALL.
     DON'T LET GO!

THE END

SAMUEL FRENCH STAFF

Nate Collins
President

Ken Dingledine
Director of Operations,
Vice President

Bruce Lazarus
Executive Director

Rita Maté
Director of Finance

ACCOUNTING

Lori Thimsen | Director of Licensing Compliance
Nehal Kumar | Senior Accounting Associate
Josephine Messina | Accounts Payable
Helena Mezzina | Royalty Administration
Joe Garner | Royalty Administration
Jessica Zheng | Accounts Receivable
Andy Lian | Accounts Receivable
Zoe Qiu | Accounts Receivable
Charlie Sou | Accounting Associate
Joann Mannello | Orders Administrator

CUSTOMER SERVICE AND LICENSING

Brad Lohrenz | Director of Licensing Development
Billie Davis | Licensing Service Manager
Fred Schnitzer | Business Development Manager
Sara Mirowski | Amateur Licensing Supervisor
Melody Fernandez | Amateur Licensing Supervisor
Laura Lindson | Professional Licensing Supervisor
Kim Rogers | Licensing Development Associate
John Tracey | Professional Licensing Associate
Matthew Akers | Amateur Licensing Associate
Jay Clark | Amateur Licensing Associate
Alicia Grey | Amateur Licensing Associate
Ashley Byrne | Amateur Licensing Associate
Jake Glickman | Amateur Licensing Associate
Chris Lonstrup | Amateur Licensing Associate
Jabez Zuniga | Amateur Licensing Associate
Glenn Halcomb | Amateur Licensing Associate

EDITORIAL AND PUBLICATIONS

Lysna Marzani | Director of Business Affairs
Amy Rose Marsh | Literary Manager
Katie Lupica | Editorial Associate
Gene Sweeney | Graphic Designer
David Geer | Publications Supervisor
Charlyn Brea | Publications Associate
Doug Katsaros | Musical Coordinator

MARKETING

Abbie Van Nostrand | Director of Marketing
Katy DiSavino | Marketing Manager
Alison Sundstrom | Marketing Associate

OPERATIONS

Joe Ferreira | Product Development Manager
Casey McLain | Operations Supervisor
Danielle Heckman | Office Coordinator, Reception

SAMUEL FRENCH BOOKSHOP (LOS ANGELES)

Cory DeLair | Bookstore Buyer
Jennifer Palumbo | Customer Service Associate
Sonya Wallace | Bookstore Associate
Tim Coultas | Bookstore Associate
Monté Patterson | Bookstore Associate
Alfred Contreras | Shipping & Receiving

LONDON OFFICE

Felicity Barks | Submissions Associate
Steve Blacker | Bookshop Associate
David Bray | Customer Services Associate
Zena Choi | Professional Licensing Associate
Robert Cooke | Assistant Buyer
Stephanie Dawson | Amateur Licensing Associate
Simon Ellison | Retail Sales Manager
Jason Felix | Royalty Administration
Susan Griffiths | Amateur Licensing Associate
Robert Hamilton | Amateur Licensing Associate
Lucy Hume | Publications Associate
Nasir Khan | Management Accountant
Simon Magniti | Royalty Administration
Louise Mappley | Amateur Licensing Associate
James Nicolau | Despatch Associate
Martin Phillips | Librarian
Zubayed Rahman | Despatch Associate
Steve sanderson | Royalty Administration Supervisor
Roger Sheppard | I.T. Manager
Geoffrey Skinner | Company Accountant
Peter Smith | Amateur Licensing Associate
Garry Spratley | Customer Service Manager
David Webster | UK Operations Director

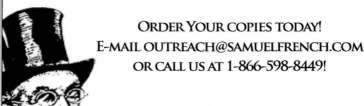